Thomas Churchyard

The Worthines of Wales

Thomas Churchyard

The Worthines of Wales

ISBN/EAN: 9783337329730

Printed in Europe, USA, Canada, Australia, Japan

Cover: Foto ©Andreas Hilbeck / pixelio.de

More available books at **www.hansebooks.com**

THE
Worthines
of VVales:

VVherein are more then a thousand seuerall things
rehearsed : some set out in prose to the pleasure of the
Reader , and with such varietie of verse for the
beautifying of the Book, as no doubt shal
delight thousands to vnderstand.

Which worke is enterlarded with many wonders and right strange
matter to consider of: All the which labour and deuice is
drawne forth and set out by Thomas Church-
yard, *to the glorie of God, and honour of*
his Prince and Countrey.

¶Imprinted at London, by G.
Robinson, for Thomas Cadman.
1587.

To the Queenes

moſt Excellent Maieſtie, Elizabeth,
by the grace of God, Queene of England,
Fraunce and Ireland, &c. Thomas Churchyard wiſheth alwayes bleſſednes, good fortune,
victorie, and worldly honour, with the encreaſe
of quiet raigne, vertuous lyfe, and moſt
Princely gouernment.

MOST *Redoubted and Royall
Queene, that Kings doe feare,
Subiects doe honour, ſtrangers
ſeeke ſuccour of, and people of
ſpeciall ſpirit acknowledge (as
their manifold books declare)
I leaſt of all, preſume to farre,
ither in preſenting matter to be iudged of, or to ad-
uenture the cracking of credite , with writing any
thing, that may breede miſlike (preſents not well taken) in the deepe iudgement of ſo high and mightie
a Princeſſe. But where a multitude runnes forward
(forced through deſire or fortune) to ſhewe ductie,
or to ſee what falleth out of their forwardnes, I ſtep-
ping in among the reſt, am driuen and led (by affec-*

* 2   *tion*

tion to followe)beyond the force of my power or feeling of any learned arte. So being thruſt on with the
throng, I finding my ſelf brought before the preſence
of your Maieſtie (.but barely furniſhed of knowledge)to whom I muſt vtter ſome matter of delight,
or from whom I muſt retourne all abaſhed with open
diſgrace. Thus Gracious Lady, vnder your Princely fauour I haue vndertaken to ſet foorth a worke
in the honour of VVales, where your highnes aunce-
ſtors tooke name , and where your Maieſtie is as
much loued and feared, as in any place of your highneſſe dominion. And the loue and obedience of which
people ſo exceedes, and ſurpaſſeth the common goodwill of the worlde , that it ſeemeth a wonder in our
age (wherein are ſo many writers)that no one man
doth not worthely according to the countries goodnes ſet forth that noble Soyle and Nation. Though
in deede diuers haue ſleightly written of the ſame,
and ſome of thoſe labours deſerueth the reading, yet
except the eye be a witnes to their workes, the writers can not therein ſufficiently yeeld due commen-
dation to thoſe ſtately Soyles and Principalities.
For which cauſe I haue trauayled ſondry times of
purpoſe through the ſame, and what is written of I
haue beheld, and throughly ſeene , to my great con-
tentment

tentment and admiration. For the *Citties, Townes,*
and goodly *Castles* thereof are to be mufed on, and
merites to bee regiſtred in euerlaſting memorie,
but chiefly the *Caſtles* (that ſtand like a company
of *Fortes*)may not be forgotten, their buyldings are
ſo princely, their ſtrength is ſo greate, and they are
ſuch ſtately ſeates and defences of nature. To which
Caſtles great Royaltie and liuings belongeth, and
haue bene and are in the giftes of Princes, now poſſeſſed of noble men and ſuch as they appoint to keep
them. The royalties whereof are alwayes looked vnto, but the Caſtles doe dayly decay, a ſorrowfull ſight
and in a maner remediles. But nowe to come to the
côditions of the people, & to ſhew ſomewhat of their
curteſie, loyalty, & naturall kindnes, I preſume your
Maieſtie will pardon me to ſpeake of, for of trueth
your highnes is no ſoner named among them, but
ſuch a generall reioyſing doth ariſe, as maketh glad
any good mans hart to behold or heare it, it proceeds
of ſuch an affectionate fauour.   For let the meaneſt
of the Court come downe to that countrey, he ſhalbe
ſo ſaluted, halſed and made of, as though he were
ſome Lords ſonne of that ſoyle, & further the plain
people thinks it debt & duetie, to follow a ſtrangers
Stirrop (being out of the way) to bring him where

The Epiſtle

he wiſheth, which gentlenes in all countries is not
vſed, and yet beſides all this goodnes and great regard, there is neither hewe nor cry (for a robbery)
in many hundreth myles riding, ſo whether it be for
feare of iuſtice, loue of God, or good diſpoſition, ſmall
Robberies or none at all are heard of there. They
triumph likewiſe ſo much of fidelitie, that the very
name of a falſifier of promes, a murtherer or a theef,
is moſt odious among them, eſpecially a Traytor is
ſo hated, that his whole race is rated at and abhord
as I haue heard there, report of Parrie and others,
who the common people would haue torne in peeces
if the lawe had not proceeded. And ſuch regard they
haue one of another, that neither in market townes,
high wayes, meetings, nor publicke aſſemblies they
ſtriue not for place, nor ſhewe any kind of royſting:
for in ſted of ſuch high ſtomackes and ſtoutnes, they
vſe frendly ſalutations and courteſie, acknowled-
ging duetie thereby, & doing ſuch reuerence to their
betters, that euery one in his degree is ſo well vn-
derſtood and honored, that none can iuſtly ſay hee
hath ſuffered iniurie, or found offence by the rude &
burbarous behauiour of the people. Theſe vſages of
theirs, with the reſt that may be ſpoken of their ciuil
maner and honeſt frame of lyfe, doth argue there is
ſome

Dedicatorie

*some more nobler nature in that Nation, then is ge-
nerally reported, which I doubt not but your Highnes is as willing to heare as I am desirous to make
manifest and publish : the hope whereof redoubleth
my boldnes, and may happely sheeld me from the ha-
zard of worlds hastie iudgement, that condemnes
men without cause for writing that they know, and
praysing of people before their faces : (which suspi-
cious heads call a kind of adulation) but if telling of
troth, be rebukable, and playne speeches be offensiue,
the ignorant world shall dwell long in errors, and
true writers may sodaynly sit in silence. J haue not
only searched sondry good Authors for the confir-
mation of my matter, but also paynfully traueiled to
trye out the substance of that is written, for feare of
committing some vnpardonable fault and offence,
in presenting this Booke vnto your Highnesse.
VVhich worke, albeit it is but litle, (because it trea-
teth not of many Shieres) yet greatly it shal reioyce
the whole Countrey of VVales, whē they shall heare
it hath found fauour in your gracious sight, & hath
passed through those blessed hands, that holds the
rayne and bridle of many a stately Kingdome, and
Terrytorie. And my selfe shall reape so much gladnesse, by the free passage of this simple labour, that*

here-

The Epistle

hereafter J shall goe through (GOD sparing life)
with the rest of the other Shieres not heere named.
These things only taken in hād, to cause your Highnesse to knowe, what puysance and strength such a
Princesse is of, that may commaund such a people:
and what obedience loue and loyaltie is in such a
Countrey, as hereunto hath bin but little spoken of,
and yet deserueth most greatest lawdation. And in
deede the more honorable it is, for that your Highnesse princely Aunceftors sprong forth of the noble
braunches of that Nation. Thus duetifully pray-
ing for your Maiesties long preseruation, (by whose
bountie and goodnesse I a long while haue liued)
J wish your Highnesse all the hap, honour,
victorie, and harts ease, that can
be desired or imagined.

Your Highnesse humble Seruant and
Subiect, Thomas Churchyard.

To euery louing and
friendly Reader.

T may feeme ftraunge (good Rea-
der) that I haue chofen in the end
of my daies to trauaile , and make
difcription of Countries : whereas
the beginning of my youth (and a
long while after) I haue haûted the
warres , and written fomewhat of
Martiall Difcipline : but as euery
feafon breedeth a feuerall humour,
and the humours of men are diuers:(drawing the mynd to
fondrie difpofitions) fo common occafion that commands
the iudgement, hath fet me a worke , and the warme good
will & affe&ion,borne in breaft,towards the worthie Countrey of Wales,hath haled me often forward, to take this labour in hand , which many before haue learnedly handled.
But yet to fhewe a difference in writing, and a playnneffe in
fpeech(becaufe playne people affe&s no florifhing phrafe)I
haue now in as ample a maner (without borrowed termes)
as I could , declared my opinion of that fweete Soyle and
good Subie&s therof,euen at that very inftant,when Wales
was almoft forgotten , or fcarce remembred with any great
lawdation , when it hath merited to be written of: for fondrie famous caufes moft meete to be honored,and neceffary
to be touched in. Firft,the world will confeffe (or els it fhall
do wrong)that fome of our greateft Kings (that haue conquered much)were borne & bred in that Countrey : which
Kings in their times,to the glory of England,haue wrought
wonders,& brought great benefites to our weale publicke.
Among the fame Princes, I pray you giue me leaue to place
our good Queene Elizabeth,and pardô me withall to com-

A   mit

mit you to the Chronicles , for the feeking out of her Aunceftors noble actions , and fuffer me to fhewe a little of the
goodneffe , gathered by vs , from her Maiefties well doing,
and poffeffed a long feafon from her princely and iuft dealings. An act fo noble & notorious , that neither can efcape
immortall fame, nor fhall not paffe my pen vnrefited.

Now weigh in what plight was our ftate when fhe came
firft to the Crowne , and fee how foone Religion was refor-
med, (a matter of great moment) peace planted, and warres
vtterly extinguifhed, as the fequell yet falleth out.

Then behold how fhe fuccoured the afflicted in *Fraunce*,
(let the going to *Newhauen* beare witneffe) and chargeably
without breaking of League mainteyned her friends and a-
mazed her enemies.

Then looke into the feruice and preferuation of *Scotland*
(at the fiege of *Leeth*) and fee how finely the French were al
fhipped away (they being a great power) and fent home in
fuch fort, that neuer fince they had mynd to returne thether
againe , in that fafhion and forme that they fayled towards
Scotland at the firft.

Then confider how bace our money was, & in what fhort
tyme (with little loffe to our Countrey) the bad coyne was
conuerted to good filuer : and fo is like to continue to the
end of the world.

Then in the aduancing of Gods word and good people,
regard how *Rochell* was relieued, and *Rome* and other places
foūd caufe to pray for her life, who fought to purchace their
peace and fee them in fafetie.

Then thinke on the care fhe tooke for *Flaunders* , during
the firft troubles , and how that Countrey had bene vtterly
deftroyed, if her Highnes helping hand had not propped vp
that tottering State.

Then Chriftianly cōceiue how many multitudes of ftran-
gers fhe hath giuen gracious countenance vnto , and hath
freely licenfed them to liue here in peace and reft.

Then paife in an equall ballance the daungerous eftate of
Scotland once againe , when the Kings owne Subiects kept
the

the Caſtle of *Edenbrough* againſt their owne naturall Lord
& Maiſter:which preſumptuous part of Subieɑs,her Highneſſe could not abide to behold: wherevpon ſhe ſent a ſuffi-
cient power to ayde the Kings Maieſtie : which power vali-
antly wonne the Caſtle,and freely deliuered the ſame to the
right owner thereof ,.with all the treaſure and priſoners.
therein.

Then regard how honourably ſhe hath dealt with diuers
Princes that came to ſee her,or needed her magnificét ſup-
portation and countenance.

Then looke throughly into the mightineſſe & managing
of all matters gone about and put in exerciſe princely, and
yet peaceably ſince the day of her Highneſſe Coronation,
and you ſhalbe forced to confeſſe that ſhe ſurmounts a great
number of her Predeceſſors : and ſhe is not at this day no
whit inferiour to the greateſt Monarke of the world.

Is not ſuch a peereles Queene then,a comfort to Wales,
a glorie to England , and a great reioyſing to all her good
neighbours? And doth not ſhe daily deſerue to haue bookes
dedicated in the higheſt degree of honor to her Highneſſe?
Yes vndoubtedly , or els my ſences and iudgement fayleth
me.

So(good Reader)do iudge of my labours:my pen is pro-
cured by a band of cauſes to write as farre as my knowledge
may leade:and my ductie hath no end of ſeruice , nor no li-
mits are ſet to a loyall Subieɑ,but to wiſh and worke to the
vttermoſt of power.

Within this worke are ſeuerall diſcourſes : ſome of the
beautie & bleſſednes of the Countrey: ſome of the ſtrength
and ſtatelyneſſe of their inpregnable Caſtles: ſome of their
trim Townes and fine ſituation : ſome of their antiquitie,
ſhewing from what Kings and Princes they tooke their firſt
name and prerogatiue.So generally of all maner of matters
belonging to that Soyle, as Churches, Monuments,Moun-
taynes,Valleys,Waters,Bridges, fayre Gentlemens houſes,
and the reſt of things whatſoeuer , may become a writers
pen to touch,or a readers iudgement to knowe. I write not

William Malmesburie de regibus anglorum. Dauid Powell a late writer, yet excellently learned, made a sharp inuectiue against William Paruus and Pollidor Virgill (& all their complices) accusing them of lying tongues, enuyous detraction, malicious slaunders, reproachfull and venomous language, wilfull ignorāce, dogged enuie, and canckered mindes, for that thei spake vnreuerently of Arthur, and many other thrise noble Princes. Iefirey of Monmouth. Matthewe of Westminster, and others are here in like sort to be read & looked on.

contenciously to find fault with any, or confute the former writers and tyme: but to aduaunce and winne credite to the present trueth, agreeing and yeelding to all former tymes and ages, that hath iustly giuen euery Nation their due, and truely without affection hath set downe in plaine words the worthines of plaine people: for I honor and loue as much a true Author, as I hate and detest a reporter of trifeling fables. A true Historie is called the Mistresse of life: and yet all Historyographers in writing of one thing, agree not well one with another: because the writers were not present in the tymes, in the places, nor saw the persons they make mētion of: but rather haue leaned and listned on the common report, than stayed or trusted to their owne experience.

Strabo a most famous writer findes fault (for the like occasion) with *Erstaotheus, Metrodorus, Septius, Possidonius,* and *Patrocles* the Geographer: And such discord did arise amóg writers in tyme past, as *Iosephus* saith against *Appio,* that they reprooued one another by bookes, and all men in generall reprooued *Herodotus.*

God shield me from such caueling: for I deliuer but what I haue seene and read: alledging for defence both auncient Authors, and good tryall of that is written. Wherefore (louing Reader) doe rather struggle with those two strong pillars of knowledge, than striue with the weaknesse of my inuention: which to auoyde sharpnesse (and bitter words) is sweetned and seasoned with gentle verses, more pleasant to some mens eares then prose, and vnder whose smooth grace of speech, more acceptable matter is conuayed, then the common sort of people can comprehend. For verses like a familiar friend (with a gallant phrase) rides quietly by thousands, and dasheth no one person, and galloping cleanly away merites no rebuke: when prose with a soft pace cannot with such cunning passe vnperceiued. But albis one when in neither of both is found no matter of mistrust, nor speeches to offend, there is no cause of dislike. So crauing thy good opinion, good Reader farewell.

A true note of the

auncient Castles, famous Monu-
ments, goodly *Riuers*, *faire Bridges*,
fine Townes, and courteous people,
that I haue seene in the noble
Countrie of *Wales*.

Hrough sondrie Soyles, and stately
Kingdomes ritch,
Long haue I traest, to tread out time
and peares:
Where I at will, haue surely seene
right mutch,
As by my works, and printed bookes
appeares.
And wearied thus, with toyle in for
rayne place,

The Authors
troublesome
life briefly
set downe.

I homeward driue, to take some rest a space:
But labouring mynd, that rests not but in bed,
Began afresh, to trouble restles hed.

Then newfound toyles, that hales men all in haste,
To runne on head, and looke not where they goe:
Bade reason ride, where loue should be enbraste,
And where tyme could, his labour best bestowe.
To Wales (quoth Wit), there doth plaine people dwell,
So mayst thou come, to heauen out of hell:
For Fraunce is fine, and full of faithlesse waies,
Poore Flaunders grosse, and farre from happie daies.

Ritch Spayne is proude, and sterne to straungers all,
In Italie, popsing is alwaies rife:

A short note
of the nature
of many Coû-
tries, with the
disposition of
the people
there.

B   And

And Germanie, to Drunkennesse doth fall,
The Danes likewise, doe leade a bibbing life.
The Scots seeke bloud, and beare a cruell mynd,
Ireland growes nought, the people waxe vnkynd:
England God wot, hath learnde such leawdnesse late,
That Wales methinks, is now the soundest state.

A commen-
dation of the
loyaltie of
Welshmen.

In all the rest, of Kingdomes farre or nere,
A tricke or two, of treacherie staynes the Soyle:
But since the tyme, that rule and lawe came here,
This Brittish land, was neuer put to foyle,
For foule offence, or fault it did commit:
The people here, in peace doth quiet sit,
Obayes the Prince, without reuolt or iarre,
Because they know, the smart of Ciuill warre.

A rehearsall of
great strife and
dissention that
ruinated
Wales.

Whiles quarrels rage, did nourish rune and wracke,
And Owen Glendore, set bloodie broyles abroach:
Full many a Towne, was spoyld and put to sacke,
And cleane consum'd, to Countries foule reproach.
Great Castles raste, fayre Buyldings burnt to dust,
Such reuell raignde, that men did liue by lust:
But since they came, and peeled vnto Lawe,
Most meeke as Lambe, within one poke they drawe.

How Lawe
and loue links
men together
like brethren.

Like brethren now, doe Welshmen still agree,
In as much loue, as any men aliue:
The friendship there, and concord that I see,
I doe compare, to Bees in Honey hiue.
Which keepe in swarme, and hold together still,
Yet gladly showe, to straunger great good will:
A courteous kynd, of loue in euery place,
A man may finde, in simple peoples face.

The accusto-
med courtesie
of Wales.

Passe where you please, 'on Plaine or Mountaine wilde,
And beare your selfe, in sweete and ciuill sort:

And

# of Wales.

And you shall sure, be haulst with man and childe,
Who will salute, with gentle comely port
The passers by: on braues they stand not so,
Without good speech, to let a trau'ler go:
They thinke it dett, and duetie franke and free,
In Towne or fielde, to'yæld you cap and knee.

They will not striue, to royst and take the way,
Of any man, that trauailes through their Land:
A greater thing, of Wales now will I say,
Ye may come there, beare purse of gold in hand,
Or mightie bagges, of siluer stuffed throwe,
And no one man, dare touch your treasure now:
Which shewes some grace, doth rule and guyde them there,
That doth to God, and man such Conscience beare.

No such theft
and robberie
in Wales as in
other Coun-
tries.

Behold besides, a further thing to note,
The best cheape cheare, they haue that may be found:
The shot is great, when each mans paies his groate,
If all alike, the reckoning runneth round.
There market good, and victuals nothing deare,
Each place is filde, with plentie all the yeare:
The ground mannurde, the graine doth so encrease,
That thousands liue, in wealth and blessed peace.

Victuals good
cheape in most
part of Wales.

But come againe, vnto their courteous shoe,
That wins the hearts, of all that markes the same:
The like whereof, through all the world doe goe,
And scarce ye shall, finde people in such frame.
For meeke as Doue, in lookes and speech they are,
Not rough and rude, (as spitefull tongues declare)
No sure they seeme, no sooner out of shell,
(But nature shewes) they knowe good maners well.

A great re-
buke to those
that speakes
not truely of
Wales.

How can this be, that weaklings nurst so harde,
(Who barely goes, both barefoote and vncled)

Good disposi-
tion neuer
wants good
maners.

B 2   In

The worthines

In gifts of mynd, should haue so great regarde,
Except within, from birth some grace were bred.
It must be so, doe wit not me deceaue,
What nature giues, the world cannot bereaue:
In this remaines, a secrete worke deuine,
Which shewe they rise, from auncient race and line.

Good & true
Authors that
affirmes more
goodnesse in
Wales than
I write of.

In Authors old, you shall that plainly reade,
Geraldus one, and learned Geffrey two:
The third for troth, is Venerable Beade,
That many graue, and worthie workes did doe.
What needes this proofe, or genalogies here,
Their noble blood, doth by their liues appeare:
Their stately Townes, and Castles euery where,
Of their renowme, doth daily witnesse beare.

A description of Monmouth Shiere.

Two Riuers
by Mōmouth,
the one called
Monnow,
and the other
Wye.

First I begin, at auncient Monmouth now,
That stands by Wye, a Riuer large and long:
I will that Shiere, and other Shieres goe throwe,
Describe them all, or els I did them wrong:
It is great blame, to writers of our daies,
That treates of world, and giues to Wales no praise:
They rather hyde, in clowde(and cunning soyle)
That Land than peeld, right glorie to that Soyle.

King Henry
the fifth.

Neere the
Towne Sir
Charles Harbert of Troy
dwelt in a faire
Seate called
Troy.

A King of ours, was borne in Monmouth sure,
The Castle there, records the same a right:
And though the walles, which cannot still endure,
Through sore decay, shewes nothing fayre to sight.
In Seate it selfe, (and well plaste Citie old)
By view ye may, a Princely plot behold:

# of Wales.

Good mynds they had, that first those walles did raise,
That makes our age, to thinke on elders daies.

The King here borne, did proue a péereles Prince,
He conquerd Fraunce, and raign'd nine péeres in hap:
There was not here, so great a Victor since,
That had such chaunce, and Fortune in his lap.
For he by fate, and force did couet all,
And as turne came, stroke hard at Fortunes ball:
With manly mynd, and ran a reddie way,
To lose a ioynt, or winne the Gole by play.

If Monmouth bring, such Princes forth as this,
A Soyle of grace, it shalbe calde of right:
Speake what you can, a happie Seate it is,
A trim Shiere towne, for Noble, Barron or Knight.
A Cittie sure, as free as is the best,
Where Size is kept, and learned Lawyers rest:
Buylt auncient wise, in swéete and wholesome ayre,
Where the best sort, of people oft repayre.

Not farre from thence, a famous Castle fine,
That Raggland hight, stands moted almost round:
Made of Fréestone, vpright as straight as line,
Whose workmanship, in beautie doth abound.
The curious knots, wrought all with edged toole,
The stately Tower, that lokes ore Pond and Pole:
The Fountaine trim, that runs both day and night,
Doth péeld in showe, a rare and noble sight.

Now Chepstowe comes, to mynd (as well it may)
Whose Seate is set, some part vpon an hill:
And through the Towne, to Neawport lyes a way,
That ore a Bridge, on Wye you ride at will.
This Bridge is long, the Riuer swift and great,
The Mountaine bigge, about doth shade the Seate:

B 3

The

Marginal notes:

At Wynestow now dwels Sir Thomas Harbert, a little from the same Troy.

Maister Roger Ieames dwelt at Troy nere this Towne.

The Earle of Worcesters house and Castle. The Earle of Penbroke that was created Earle by King Edward the 4. buylt the Castell of Raggland sumptuously at the first. Earle of Worcester Lord hereof. A faire bridge. Maister Lewis of Saint Peere dwelles neere that.

The worthines

Sir Charles Sommerset at the Grange doth dwell now.

The craggie Rocks, that ore the Towne doth lye,
Of force farre of, doth hinder viewe of eye.

The common Port, and Hauen is so good,
It merits praise, because Barkes there doe ride:

Sir William Morgan that is dead dwelt at Pennycoyd.

To which the Sea, comes in with flowing flood,
And doth foure howers, aboue the Bridge abide.
Beyond the same, doth Tynterne Abbey stand,
As old a Sell, as is within that Land:

Harbet of Colbroke buryed there.
Chepstow.

Where diuers things, hath bene right worthie note,
Whereof as yet, the troth I haue not gote.

In the Castle there is an ancient tower called Longis tower, wherby rests a tale to be considered of.

To Chepstowe yet, my pen agayne must passe,
Where Strongbow once, (an Earle of rare renowne)
A long time since, the Lord and Maister was
(In princely sort) of Castle and of Towne.
Then after that, to Mowbray it befell,
Of Norffolke Duke, a worthie knowne full well:

Of this Earle is a great and worthie tale to be heard
A peece of a petigree.

Who sold the samet, o William Harbert Knight,
That was the Earle, of Penbrooke then by right.

Earle Strongbowe was maried to the King of Lynsters Daughter in Ireland, and this Strongbowe wan by force of armes the Earledoms of Wolster & Tyroll.

His eldest Sonne, that did succeede his place,
(Of Huntyngton: and Penbrooke Earle likewise)
Had but one childe, a Daughter of great race:
And she was matcht, with pompe and solempne guise,
To Somerset, that was Lord Chamberlaine,
And made an Earle, in Henry seuenths raigne:
Of him doth come, Earle Worster liuing nowe,
Who buildeth vp, the house of Raggland throwe.

A Creation of an Earle.

EDward by the grace of God, King most imperiall,
Of France, & England, & the Lord of Ireland therwithall,
To Archbishops, & Bishops all, to Abbotes and to Priors
To Dukes, to Earles, to Barrons, & to Sheriffes of the shires.
To

# of Wales.

To Iustices, to Maiors, and chiefe of Townly gouernment,
To Baylieffes, & my lichefolke all, haue herewith greeting sent.
Knowe ye whereas we iudge it is a gracious Prince his parte,
To yæld loue, fauour, and reward to men of great desarte:
Who of himselfe, his Royall house, and of the publique state,
Haue well deseru'd, their vertues rare euer to renumerate:
And to adorne with high reward, such vertue clære and bright,
Stirs others vp to great attempts, and faintnes puts to flight.
We following on the famous cóurse, y former Kings haue run,
That worthie & approued wight, whose dædes most nobly dun,
Haue greatest things of vs deseru'd, we do intend to raïse,
To fame and honors highest type, with gifts of Princely praïse,
That truely regall are we meane, that valiant worthie Knight,
That William Herbert hath to name, & now L. Herbert hight.
Whose seruice whē we first did raigne, we did most faithful find,
When for our royal right we fought, which stil we call to mind:
To which we ad from then till now, continuall seruices,
Which many were whereof each one, to vs most pleasing is.
And chiefly when as lately now, his dædes did him declare,
A worthie Knight wherby he gayn'd, both fame and glorie rare:
When as that Rebell and our foe, euen Iasper Tudyrs sonne,
who said he Earle of Penbroke was, did westwales coast oreru.
And there by subtile shifts and force, did diuers sondrie waies
Anoy our State, and therewithall a vyle Sedition raïse.
But there he gaue to him a fielde, and with a valiant hand
Orethrew him and his forces all, that on his part did stand.
And marching all along those Coasts, y most he slew out right,
The rest he brake and so disperst, they gaue themselues to flight.
Our Castle then of Hardelach, that from our first daies raigne,
A refuge for all Rebels did, against vs still remaine:
A Fort of wonderous force, besiege about did he,
And tooke it, where in most mens mynds, it could not taken be.
He wan it & did make them yæld, who there their saftie sought,
And all the Countrie thereabouts, to our obedience brought.
These therefore his most worthie Acts, we calling into minde,
His seruices and great desarts, which we praise worthie finde:

And

The worthines

And for that cause we willing him, with honors royally
For to adorne, decke, and aduaunce, and to sublime on hye,
The eight day of September, in the eight yéere of our Raigne,
We by this Charter, that for ours shall firme for euer remaine:
Of speciall grace and knowledge sure, sound and determinate,
And motió méere him William doe, of Penbroke Count create
Erect, preferre, and vnto him the Title stile and state,
And name thereof and dignitie, foreuer appropriate,
As Earle of Penbroke and withall, we giue all rights that do
All honors and preheminence, that state perteyne vnto:
With which estate, stile, honor, great, and worthie dignitie,
By cincture of a Sword, we him ennoble reallie.

The Authors verses in the honor of noble mynds.
For that the sence, and worthie words were great,
The seruice such, as merites noble fame:
The forme thereof, in verse J doe repeate,
And shewe likewise, the Lattin of the same.
He seru'd a King, that could him well reward,
And of his house, and race tooke great regard,
And recompenst, his manly doing right,
With honor due, to such a noble Knight.

Good men are made of, and bad men rebuked.
Where loyall mynd, doth offer life and all,
For to preserue, the Prince and publique state:
There doth great hap, and thankfull Fortune fall,
As guerdon sent, by destinie and good fate.
No Soueraine can, forget a Subiects troeth,
With whose good grace, great loue and fauour goeth:
Great gifts and place, great glorie and renowne,
They get and gayne, that truely serues a Crowne.

Sir William Harbert of Saint Gillyans.
And thou my Knight, that art his heire in blood,
Though Lordship, land, and Ragglands stately towers,
A female heire, and force of fortunes flood
Haue thée bereft, yet bearst his fruits and flowers:

His

His armes, his name, his faith and mynd are thyne,
By nature, nurture, arte and grace deuyne:
Ore Seas and Lands, these moue thee paynes to take,
For God, for fame, for thy sweete Soueraines sake.

❧ Here followeth the Creation
of an Earle of Penbroke in Latin.

Edwardus Dei gracia Rex Anglię & Frauncię & Dominus Hibernię, Archiepiscopis, Episcopis, Abbatib°, Prioribus, Ducibus, Comitibus, Baronibus, Iusticiarijs, Vicecomitibus, Prepositis, Ministris, & omnibus Balliuis, & fidelibus suis, salutē. Sciatis quod cum felicis & grati admodum Regis munus censeamus, de se, de Regia domo, deque Republica & regno bene meritas personas, cōgruis amore, beneuolentia & liberalitate prosequi: denique & iuxta eximias probitates, easdem magnificentiùs ornare & decorare, quatenus in personis huiuscemodi congestis clarissimis virtutum pręmijs ceteri, socordia ignauiaque sepositis ad peragenda pulcherrima quæque facinora laude & gloria concitentur: Nos ne à maiorum nrō laudatissimis moribus discedere videamur, nostri esse officij putamus probatissimū nobis virum qui ob res ab se clarissimè gestas quàm maxima de nobis promeruit, condignis honorū fastigijs attollere & verè regijs insignire muneribus. Strennum & insignem loquimur militē Willūm Herbert Dominum Herbart, iam defunctū, cuius in regni nostri primordijs obsequia gratissima tum nobis multipliciter impensa cum nrō pro iure decertaretur, satis ambiguè obliuisci non possumus accessere & de post in hoc vsque temporis continuata seruicia, que non parum nobis fuere complacita, presertim nuperimis hijs diebus quibus optimum se gessit militem, ac non mediocres sibi laudis & fame titulos comparauit. Hijs equidem iampridē cū Rebellis, hostisque nostri Iasper Owini Tedur filliū, nuper Pembrochiæ se Comitem dicens, Walliæ partes peruaderet,

C

uaderet, multaque arte ad contra nos & statum nostrum vilem populo seditionem concitandum truculentiam moliretur, societatis sibi ad eandem rem conficiendam electissimis viris fidelibus nostris arma cepit, confligendi copiam hostibus exhibuit, adeoque valida manu peruasus ab ipsis partes peruagatus est & nusquam eis locum permiserit quo nó eos complicesque affligauerit, vires eorúdem fregerit, morteque affecerit, seu desperantes in fugam propulerit, demum Castrum nostrum de Hardelagh nobis ab initio regni nostri contrarium, quo vnicum miseris patebat refugium, obsidione vallabat, quod capi impossible ferebatur, cepit, inclusos que ad deditionem compulit, adiacentem quoq; primam omnem nostram Regiæ Maiestati rebellem hactenus ad summam obedientiam reduxit. Hæc itaque sua laudabilia obsequia, promeritaque memoriter & vt decet intimè recolentes volentesque proinde eundem Willúm condignis honoribus, regalibúsque præmijs ornare amplicare & sublimare, octauo die Septembris anno regni nostri octauo, per Chartam nostram de gratia nostra speciali ac ex certa scientia & mero motu nostris ipsum Willúm in Comitem Pembrochiæ ereximus, præfecerimus, & creauerimus, & ei nomé, statum, stilum, titulum, & dignitatem Comitis Pembrochie cum omnibus & singulis preëminencijs honoribus & ceteris quibuscunque huius statui Comitis pertinentibus, siue congruis dederimus & concesserimus, ipsumq; huiusmodi statu, stilo, titulo, honore, & dignitate per cincturam gladij insigniuerimus, & realiter nobilitauerimus.

This was set downe, for causes moze then one,
The wozld belæues, no moze than it hath seene:
When things lye dead, and tyme is past and gone,
Blynd people say, it is not so we weene.
It is a tale, deuisde to please the eare,
Moze foz delight, of topes then troth may beare:
But those that thinks, this may a fable be,
To Authozs good, I send them here from me.

Fiiii

First let them search, Records as J haue done,
Then shall they finde, this is most certaine true:
And all the rest, before J here begun,
Js taken out, not of no writers nue.
The oldest sort, and soundest men of skill
Myne Authors are, now reade their names who will:
Their workes, their words, and so their learning through,
Shall shewe you all, what troth J write of now.

BEcause many that fauoured not Wales (parsiall writers and
historians) haue written & set downe their owne opinions, as
they pleased to publish of that Countrey: J therefore a little de-
gresse from the orderly matter of the booke, and touch somewhat
the workes and wordes of them that rashly haue written more
then they knewe, or well could proue.

As learned men, hath wrote graue works of yore,
So great regard, to natiue Soyle they had:
For such respect, J blame now Pollydore:
Because of Wales, his iudgement was but bad.
Jf Buckanan , the Scottish Poet late
Were here in sprite, of Brittons to debate:
He should finde men, that would with him dispute,
And many a pen, which would his works confute.

But with the dead, the quick may neuer striue,
(Though sondrie works, of theirs were little worth)
Yet better farre, they had not bene aliue,
Than sowe such seedes, as brings no goodnesse forth:
Their praise is small, that plucks backe others fame,
Their loue not great, that blots out neighbours name,
Their bookes but brawles, their bable bauld and bare,
That in disdaine, of fables writers are.

What fable more, then say they knowe that thing
They neuer sawe, and so giue iudgement streight:

And

The worthines

And by their bookes, the world in error bring,
That thinks it reades, a matter of great weight.
When that a tale, of much vntroth is told:
Thus all that shines, and glisters is not gold:
Nor all the bookes, that auncient Fathers wrate
Are not alo'wd, for troth in euery state.

Though Cæsar was, a wise and worthie Prince,
And conquerd much, of Wales and England both:
The writers than, and other Authors since,
Did flatter tyme, and still abuse the troth.
Some for a fee, and some did humors feede,
When fore was healde, to make a wound to bleede:
And some sought meanes, their patient still to please,
When body throwe, was full of foule disease.

The worldly wits, that with each tyme would wagge,
Were carped cleane, away from wisedomes lore:
They rather watcht, to fill an emptie bagge,
Than touch the tyme, then present or before:
Nor car'd not much, for future tyme to come,
They could vp tyme, like threede about the thome:
And when their clue, on trifles all was spent,
Much rotten stuffe, vnto the garment went.

Which stuffe patcht vp, a péece of homely ware,
In Printers shop, set out to sale sometyme:
Which ill wrought worke, at length became so bare,
It neither seru'd, for prose nor pleasant ryme:
But past like chat, and old wiues tales full vayne,
That thunders long, but neuer brings forth rayne:
A kynd of sound, that makes a hurling noyse,
To feare young babes, with brute of bugges and toyes.

But aged sires, of riper wit and skill,
Disdaines to reade, such rabble farst with lyes:

This

This is enough, to shewe you my goodwill
Of Authors true, and writers graue and wise.
Whose pen shall proue, each thing iu printed booke,
Whose eyes withall, on matter straunge did looke:
And whose great charge, and labour witnesse beares,
Their words are iust, they offer to your eares.

Each Nation had, some writer in their daies
For to aduaunce, their Countrey to the Starres:
Homer was one, who gaue the Greekes great praise,
And honord not, the Troyans for their warres.
Liui among, the Romaines wrate right mitch,
With rare renowne, his Countrey to enritch:
And Pollidore, did ply the pen a pace,
To blurre straunge Soyles, and yeld the Romaines grace.

Admit they wrate, their volumes all of troeth,
(And did affect, ne mian nor matter then)
Yet writer sees, not how all matters goeth
In field: when he, at home is at his pen.
This Pollidore, sawe neuer much of Wales,
Though he haue told, of Brittons many tales:
Cæsar himself, a Victor many a way,
Went not so farre, as Pollidore doth say.

Kings are obayd, where they were neuer seene,
And men may write, of things they heare by eare:
So Pollidore, oft tymes might ouerwæne,
And speake of Soyles, yet he came neuer there.
Some runne a ground, that through each water sailes,
A Pylot good, in his owne Compasse failes:
A writer that beleeues in worlds report,
May roue to farre, or surely shoote to short.

The eye is iudge, as Lanterne clære of light,
That searcheth through, the dim and darkest place:

C 3   The

The worthines

The gladſome eye, giues all the bodie ſight,
It is the glaſſe, and beautie of the face.
But where no face, nor iudging eye doth come,
The ſence is blynd, the ſpirit is deaffe and domb:
For wit can not, conceiue till ſight ſend in
Seme ſkill to head, whereby we knowledge win.

If ſtraungers ſpeake, but ſtraungely on our ſtate,
Thinke nothing ſtraunge, though ſtraungers write amis:
If ſtraungers do, our natiue people hate,
Our Countrey knowes, how ſtraunge their nature is.
Moſt ſtraunge it were, to truſt a forayne foe,
Or fauour thoſe, that me for ſtraungers knowe:
Then ſtraungely reade, the bookes that ſtraungers make,
For feare ye ſhroude, in boſome ſtinging Snake.

Poli.dorus Virgilius ſpake all of his owne nations praiſe, and ſawe but little of Brittaine, nor loued the ſame.

The ſtraungers ſtill, in auncient tyme that wrate,
Exalt themſelues, and keepes vs vnder foote:
As we of kynd, and nature doe them hate,
So beare they ruſt, and canker at the roote
Of heart, to vs, when pen to paper goeth,
Their cunning can, with craft ſo cloke a troeth,
That hardly we, ſhall haue them in the winde,
To ſmell them forth, or yet their fineneſſe finde.

Venerable Bede, a noble writer.

Gildas, a paſſing Poet of Brittaine.

Of force then muſt, you credite our owne men,
(Whoſe vertues works, a glorious garland gaynes)
Who had the gift, the grace and arte of pen:
And who did write, with ſuch ſweete flowing vaynes,
That Honey ſeem'd, to drop from Poets quill:
I ſay no more, truſt ſtraungers and ye will,
Our Countrey breedes, as faithfull men as thoſe,
As famous to, in ſtately verſe or proſe.

Sibilla, a deuine Propheſiar & writer.

And trueth I trowe, is likte among vs beſt:
For each man frounes, when fabling toyes they heare,

And

And though we count, but Robin Hood a Iest,
And old wiues tales, as tatling toyes appeare:
Yet Arthurs raigne, the world cannot denye,
Such proofe there is, the troth thereof to trye:
That who so speakes, against so graue a thing,
Shall blush to blot, the fame of such a King.

Condemne the daies, of elders great or small,
And then blurre out, the course of present tyme:
Cast one age downe, and so doe orethrow all,
And burne the bookes, of printed prose or ryme:
Who shall beleeue, he rules or she doth raigne
In tyme to come, if writers loose their paine:
The pen records, tyme past and present both,
Skill brings foorth bookes, and bookes is nurse to troth.

Now followes the Castles and
Townes neere Oske, and
there aboutes.

A Prety Towne, calde Oske neere Raggland stands,
A Riuer there, doth beare the selfesame name:
His Christall streames, that runnes along the Sands,
Shewes that it is, a Riuer of great fame.
Fresh water sweete, this goodly Riuer yeelds,
And when it swels, it spreads ore all the Feelds:
Great store of Fish, is caught within this flood,
That doth in deede, both Towne and Countrey good.

A thing to note, when Sammon failes in Wye,
(And season there: goes out as order is)
Than still of course, in Oske doth Sammons lye,
And of good Fish, in Oske you shall not mis.
And this seemes straunge, as doth through Wales appeere,
In some one place, are Sammons all the yeere:

Sa

So fresh, so sweete, so red, so crimp withall,
As man might say, loe, Sammon here at call.

King Edward
the fourth and
his children,
(as some af-
firme),and
King Richard
the third, were
borne here.

A Castle there, in Oske doth yet remaine,
A Seate where Kings, and Princes haue bene borne
It stands full ore, a goodly pleasant Plaine,
The walles whereof, and towers are all to torne,
(With wethers blast, and tyme that weares all out)
And yet it hath, a fayre prospect about:
Trim Meades and walkes, along the Riuers side,
With Bridge well built, the force of flood to bide.

Castle Scroge
doth yet re-
maine three
myle from
Oske, but the
Castle is al-
most cleane
downe.

Upon the side, of woodie hill full fayre,
This Castle stands, full sore decayde and broke:
Yet builded once, in fresh and wholesome ayre,
Full neere great Woods, and many a mightie Oke,
But sith it weares, and walles so wastes away,
In praise thereof, I mynd not much to say:
Each thing decayd, goes quickly out of minde,
A rotten house, doth but fewe fauours finde.

In the Duchie
of Lancaster,
these three
Castles are,
but not in
good plight
any way.

Three Castles fayre, are in a goodly ground,
Grosmont is one, on Hill it builded was:
Skenfreth the next, in Ualley is it found,
The Soyle about, for pleasure there doth passe.
Whit Castle is, the third of worthie fame,
The Countrey there, doth beare Whit Castles name,
A stately Seate, a loftie princely place,
Whose beautie giues, the simple Soyles some grace.

The Duke of
Yorke once
lay here, and
now the Ca-
stell is in Mai-
ster Roger
Willyams
hands.

Two myles from that, upon a mightie Hill,
Langibby stands, a Castle once of state:
Where well you may, the Countrey view at will,
And where there is, some buildings newe of late.
A wholesome place, a passing plat of ground,
As good an ayre, as there abouts is found:

Is

of Wales.

It seemes to sight, the Seate was platt so well,
In elders daies, some Duke therein did dwell.

Carleon now, step in with stately style,
No feeble phrase, may serue to set thee forth:
Thy famous Towne, was spoke of many a myle,
Thou hast bene great, though now but little worth.
Thy noble bounds, hath reacht beyond them all,
In thée hath bene, King Arthurs golden Hall:
In thée the wise, and worthies did repose,
And through thy Towne, the water ebs and flowes.

Come learned lore with loftie style,
    and leade these lynes of myne:
Come gracious Gods, and spare a whyle
    to me the Muses nyne.
Come Poets all, whose passing phrase
    doth pearce the finest wits:
Come knowledge whereon world doth gase,
    (yet still in iudgement sits)
And helpe my pen to play his parte,
    for pen is stept on stage,
To shewe by skill and cunning arte,
    the state of former age.
For present tyme hath friends enowe,
    to flatter faune and faine:
And elders daies I knowe not how,
    doe dwell in deepe disdaine.
No friend for auncient péeres we finde,
    our age loues youth alone:
The former age weares out of minde,
    as though such tyme were none.

King Arthurs raigne (though true it weare)
Is now of small account:

D   The

A description of Carleon.

Maister Morgan of Lanternam in a fayre house dwelles two mile from Carleon.

A plaine and true rehearsall of matter of great antiquitie.

A fayre Fountaine now begun.
A free Schoole now erected by Maister Morgan of Lanternam.

A gird to the flatterers and fauners of present tyme.

A house of reformatio newly begun likewise.

The Bishop of Landaffe still lying in the Towne.

We praise and extoll strange Nations, and forget or abase our owne Countries.

The fame of Troy is knowne each where,
And to the Skyes doth mount.

Both Athens, Theabes, and Carthage too
We hold of great renowne:
What then I pray you shall we do,
To poore Carleon Towne.

In Arons the Martyrs Church King Arthur was crowned.

King Arthur sure was crowned there,
It was his royall Seate:
And in that Towne did Scepter beare,
With pompe and honor greate.

Three Archbishops, Yorke London, and Carleō, crowning King Arthur.

An Archbishop that Dubrick hight,
Did crowne this King in deede:
Foure Kings before him bore in sight,
Foure golden Swords we reade.

Arthur was great, that cōmanded such solemnitie.

These Kings were famous of renowne,
Yet for their homage due:
Repayrd vnto Carleon Towne,
As I rehearse to you.

The true Authors are in the beginning of this booke for profe of this.

How many Dukes, and Earles withall,
God Authors can you tell:
And so true writers shewe you shall,
How Arthur there did dwell.

What Court he kept, what Acts he did,
What Conquest he obtaynd:
And in what Princely honor still,
King Arthur long remaynd.

Another notable solemnitie at a Coronation.

Quéene Gueneuer was crown'd likewise,
In Iulius Church they say:

Where

# of VVales.

Where that fower Quéenes in folemne guife,
(In royall rich aray).

Foure Pigeons white, boe in their hands
Before the Princeffe face:
In figne the Quéene of Brittifh **Lands**,
Was worthie of that grace.

Carleon lodged all thefe Kings,
And many a noble Knight:
As may be prou'd by fondie things,
That I haue féene in fight.

The bounds hath bene nine mples about,
The length thereof was great:
It fhewes it felf this day throughout,
It was a Princes Seate.

In Arthurs tyme a Table round,
Was there whereat he fate:
As yet a plot of goodly ground,
Sets foth that rare eftate.

The Citie reacht to Creetchurch than,
And to Saint Gillyans both:
Which yet appeares to view of man,
To trye this tale a troth.

There are fuch Uautes and hollowe Caues,
Such walles and Condits déepe:
Made all like pypes of earthen pots,
Wherein a child may créepe.

Such ftreates and pauements fondie waies,
To euery market Towne:

In Iuftus
Church the
Martyr the
Queene was
crowned.
An honor rare
and great yet
feldome feene.

A deepe and
large round
peece of groūd
fhewes yet
where Arthur
fate.

A Church on
a hil a mile of.
Saint Gillyans
is a faire houfe
where Sir Wil-
liam Harbert
dwelles.

Wonderfull
huge and long
pauements.

D 2   Such

Such Bridges built in elders daies,
And things of such renowne.

The notablest seate to behold being on the top that may be seene.

As men may muse of to behold,
But chiefly for to note:
There is a Castle very old,
That may not be forgot.

The Castle almost downe.

It stands vpon a forced Hill,
Not farre from flowing flood:
Where loe ye view long Vales at will,
Enuyron'd all with wood.

The flowing water may easily be brought about both Towne and Castle.

A Seate for any King aliue,
The Soyle it is so sweete:
Fresh springs doth streames of water bgiue,
Almost through euery streate.

A great beautie of grounds, waters, groues, & other pleasures for the eye to be seene from the old Castle of Carleon.

From Castle all these things are seene,
    as pleasures of the eye:
The goodly Groues and Vallies greene,
    and woodie Mountaines hye.
The crooked Creekes and pretie Brookes,
    that are amid the Plaine:
The flowing Tydes that spreads the land,
    and turnes to Sea againe.
The stately Wals that like a hoope,
    doth compasse all the Vale:

I haue seene Caues vnder ground (at this day) that goe I knowe not how farre, all made of excellent work, and goodly great stones both ouer head and vnder foote, &

The Princely plots that stands in troope,
    to beautifie the Dale.
The Riuers that doth daily runne,
    as cleare as Christall stone:
Shewes that most pleasures vnder Sunne,
    Carleon had alone.

Great ruth to see so braue a Soyle,
Fall in so sore decay:

                                    In

In sorowe sit, full nere the toyle,
As Fortune fled away.

And world forsooke to knowledge those,
That earst hath bene so greate:
Where Kings and graue Philosophers,
Made once therein their Seate.

Vrbs legionum was it namde,
In Cæsars daies I trowe:
And Arthur holding residence there,
(As stories plainly showe).

Not only Kings and noble Péeres,
Repayrde vnto that place:
But learned men full many yéeres,
Receiu'd therein their grace.

Than you that auncient things denyes,
Let now your talke surcease:
When profe is brought before your eyes,
Ye ought to hold your peace.

And let Carleon haue his right,
And iope his wonted fame:
And let each wise and worthie wight,
Speake well of Arthurs name.

Would God the brute thereof were knowne,
In Countrey, Court, and Towne:
And she that sits in reagall Throne,
With Scepter, Sword, and Crowne.

(Who came from Arthurs race and lyne)
Would marke these matters throwe:

dose and fine round about the whole Caue.

The name so mightie argues it was a mightie and noble towne.

Two hundred Philosophers were norished in Carleon.

Yeeld right as well to our elders daies, as to our present age.

And shewe thereon her gracious eyne,
To helpe Carleon now.

Thus farre my pen in Arthurs praise,
Hath past for plainnesse sake:
In honor of our elders daies,
That kæpes my muse awake.

All only for to publish plaine,
Tyme past, tyme present both:
That tyme to come, may well retaine,
Of each good tyme, the troth.

¶ An Introduction to the Letters sent

from *Lucius Tyberius*, at the Coro-
nation of King Arthur.

NOt vnwilling to delate and make large the matter now
written of, & further because the raigne of King Arthur
is diuersly treated on and vncertainly spoken of (the men
of this world are growen so wise) I haue searched and found (in
good Authors) such certaintie of King Arthur, and matter that
merits the reading, that I am compelled with pen to explaine,
and with some paines and studie to present the world with in generall. The substance whereof being in Latin, (may be read and
vnderstood by thousands) is englished because the common sorte
(as well as the learned) shall see how little the Kings and Princes of this Land, haue esteemed the power of the Romaines, or
manasing and force of any fortaine foe whatsoeuer. And for the
amending of my tale, let our Soueraine Ladie be well consine-
red of, (whose graces passeth my pen to shewe) and vpon that see
great things are encountred, and no small matters gone about
and brought to good passe, in the action afore named: which be-
commeth well a Quæne of that race, who is descended of so noble a progenie. But now purposing orderly to proceede to the
former

former diſcourſe, and to rehearſe word for word, as it was left by
our forefathers, (men of great learning and knowledge) I haue
ſet doune ſome ſuch Letters and Orations, as peraduenture wil
make you to maruell of, or at the leaſt to thinke on ſo much, that
ſome one among a multitude, will yéeld me thankes for my labour, and rather encourage a true writer to continue in the like
exerciſes; then to giue him any occaſion to ſit ydle, and ſo forget
the vſe of pen. There followeth hereafter thoſe things before
mentioned, which I hope the Readers will iudge with aduiſe-
ment, and conſtrue to the beſt intent and meaning. For this matter not only ſhewes by good authoritie the royall Coronation of
King Arthur, but in like maner declares with what pride and
pomp the Romains ſent hether (at the very inſtant of this great
tryumph) for tribute and homage: at which proud and preſumptuous demaund, King Arthur (and all his other Princes about
him) began to bee greatly moued, and preſently without further
delay, gaue ſo ſharpe and ſodaine an anſwer to the Embaſſadors
of Rome, that they were ſo vexed and abaſhed therewith, that
they neither knewe well how to take it, nor made any further re-
ply: as followes by matter preſently here, if you pleaſe throughly
to reade it. Conſider withall, that after this Embaſſage, King
Arthur in plaine battaile ſluc Lucius, and had gone to Rome to
haue bene crowned Emperour there, if Mordred had not made
a reuolt in Arthurs owne kingdome.

The Coronation, and ſolemnitie ther-

of: The Embaſſage, and proude meſſage of the
Romaines: And the whole reſolution of
King Arthur therein, is firſt ſet
forth here in Engliſh.

THE appoynted tyme of the ſolemnitie approching, and all
being readie aſſembled in the Citie of Carleon, the Arch-
biſhops, London and Yorke: and in the Citie of Carleon
the Archbiſhop Dubright were conueighed to the Palace, with
royall

royall solemnitie to crowne King Arthur . Dubright therefore
(because the Court then lay within his Diocesse, furnished himselfe accordingly to perfourme and solemnize this charge in his
owne person. The King being crowned, was royally brought to
the Cathedrall Church of that Metropoliticall See . On either
hand of him, both the right and the left, did two Archbishoppes
support him. And fower Kings, to wit, Angusell King of Albania, Caduall King of Venedocia , Cador King of Cornewall,
& Sater King of Demetia, went before him, carping iiii. golden
Swords. The companies also and concourse of sondrie sorts of
officers, played afore him most melodious & heauenly harmonie.
On the other parte , the Quéene was brought to the Church of
professed Nunnes, being côducted and accompanied with Archbishops and Bishops, with her Armes and titles royally garni-
shed . And the Quéeues , being wiues vnto the fower Kings a-
foresayd, carped before her (as the order and custome was) fower
white Doues or Pigeons.   10

   For behold , twelue discréete personages of reuerend countenance came to the King in stately maner , carping in their right
hands in token and signe of Ambassage, Oliue boughes. And after they had saluted him, they deliuered vnto him on the behalfe
of Lucius Tyberius, Letters contayning this effect.

¶The Epistle of Lucius the Romaine
Lieutenant, to Arthur King of Britaine .

LVcius Gouerner of the Commonwealth, to Arthur King
of Britaine, as he hath deserued . I haue excéedingly won-
dered to thinke of thy malepert and tyrannicall dealing . I
doe meruaile (I say) and in considering the matter, I am angrie
and take in ill part, the iniurie that thou hast offered to Rome:
and that thou, no better aduising thy self, refusest to acknowledge
her. Neither hast thou any care speedelie to redresse thyne ouer-
sight, thus by vniust dealings to offend the Senate: vnto whom
                                                          thou

thou art not ignorant, that the whole world oweth homage and
seruice. For, the Tribute done for Britaine which the Senate
commaunded thee to pay; for that Iulius Cæsar, and other worthie Romaines long and many yeeres enioyed the same, thou to
the contempt of such an honorable Estate, hast presumed to de-
taine and keepe backe. Thou hast also taken from them Gallia:
thou hast wonne from them, the Prouinces of Sauoy and Daul-
phinie: thou hast gotten the possession of all the Ilands of the Allobroges
Ocean: the Kings whereof (so long as the Romaine authoritie
was there obeyed)payed Tribute to our Auncestors. Sith therfore the Senate hath decreed to redemaund amends and restitu-
tion at thy hands for these thy so great wrongs, I enioyne and
commaund thee to come to Rome in the middest of August the
next yeere; there to answere vnto thy Lords, and to abyde such
sentence and order, as they by iustice shall lay vpon thee. Which
thing if thou refuse to doe, I will inuade thy Countries, and
whatsoeuer thy wilfull rashnes hath disloyally taken away from
their Commonwealth, that will I by dint of sword, assay to re-
couer and to them restore.

¶Cador the Duke of Cornewall
his Oration to the King.

I haue hitherto bene in feare, least the Britaines through much
ease and long peace, should growe to slouth and cowardize:
and lose that honorable reputation of Cheualrie and martiall
prowesse, wherein they are generally accoumpted to surmount
all other Nations. For where the vse of Armes is not esteemed,
but in steede therof, Dycing, Carding, dalying with women and
other vayne delites frequented, it cannot choose, but there cowardize and sluggardie must needes dimme and deface all vertue,
honour, valiaunce, and fame. There bee now almost fiue yeeres
passed, since we hauing lacked Martial exercise, haue effeminate-
ly bene nuzzeled in these foresayd delites. God therefore not willing to see vs any longer marred and stayned with sluggardie,

E   hath

The worthines

hath ſtirred vp the Romaines, that they ſhould be the meanes to reduce our auncient valour vnto the former ſtate and dignitie. While hee vſed theſe and ſuch like wordes, confirmed by thoſe that were there at that tyme in preſence, they came at length to their Benches or Seates, where after that euery perſon was ſet and placed; Arthur vſed this ſpǽch vnto them.

❧ The Oration of Arthur
to his Lords and people.

MY fellowes (ſayth he) and companyons both of aduerſitie and proſperitie: whoſe fidelities I haue heretofore, both in your ſound counſels, and in exployting militare ſeruices had good tryall and experience of: liſten now and aſſord vnto me your aduiſe, and wiſely foreſee, what you thinke conuenient for vs, touching ſuch demaunds and commaundements, to be done. For, when a thing is wiſely aforehand deliberated and carefully foreſeene, when it commeth to the pinch, it is more eaſilie auoyded and tolerated. We ſhall therefore the eaſier bee able to abyde the imperious demawns of Lucius, if wee lay our heads together and foreſee, how and which way, wee may beſt defeate and infringe the ſame. And (ſurely) for my part, I doe not thinke that we haue any cauſe greatly to feare him, ſith vpon an vnreaſonable cauſe he ſeeketh to haue a tribute payed out of Britaine. For, he alledgeth, that the ſame is due and payable to him, becauſe it was payd to Iulius Cæſar and others his Succeſſors, which being inuited and called hether through the diſcorde and iarres of the auncient Britaines, arriued here in Britaine with numbers of armed Souldiours: and with force and vyolence, brought vnder their ſubiection, this our Countrey, miſerably toſſed with ciuile garboyles and domeſticall diſcord. And becauſe they in this ſort, got the poſſeſſion of it, they haue ſince taken and vniuſtly receiued a Tribute out of it. For nothing that is gotten by force and vyolence, is iuſtly poſſeſſed by hun that offered the vyolence. The cauſe therefore which he pretendeth is vnreaſonable,

ble, whereby he bindeth vs by law and right to be tributarie vnto them. Sith therfore he thus presumeth to demaund of vs that
which is vniust : let vs by the same reason, demaund of him, tribute at Rome : & he that is the stronger, let him carie away that
which he desireth and claymeth . For, if his reason, why he de-
maundeth tribute now, as due, to be payed by vs, because Cæsar
and other Romaine Princes sometymes conquered Britaine be
good : by the like reason, I doe thinke that Rome ought to pay
tribute to mee , because my Predecessors heretofore wanne and
subdued it. For Belinus that most noble King of Britaines, with
the helpe and ayde of his brother Brennus Duke of Sauoy, tooke **Allobroges**
by force that Citie , and long while possessed it , hanging vp in
the middest of their chiefe Market place and high streate, twentie
of the chiefest Nobles among them. Constantine also the sonne
of Helena, and Maximianus likewise , being both of them, my
nere Cosens , and either of them successiuely , crowned King of
Britaine , were enthronized in the imperiall Seate of the Romaine Empyre. What thinke ye now? Iudge you that the Romaines haue any reason or right to demaunde Tribute at our
hands? As touching Fraunce or other collaterall Ilands of the
Ocean, it needeth no answere, sith they refused to defend them,
when we forcibly tooke them out of their cloutches & iurisdiction.

The answere of Howell King
of little Britaine.

Though euery one of you should neuer so diligently consider:
and debate with himselfe neuer so aduisedly in his mynd: yet
doe I not thinke , that he could possiblie deuise any better counsell then this, which thy most graue wisedome hath now remembred. Thy eloquent and Tullie like aduise therefore, hath furnished vs with that skill, whereby wee ought incessantly to com-
mende in you the affect of a constant man , the effect of a wise
mynd, and the benefite of prudent counsell . For, if ye will take
your voyage and expedition to Rome, according to the reason a-

C 2   fore

fore alledged, I doubt not, but wee should winne tryumph, sith wee doe but defend our libertie, and iustly demaund of our enemies, that, which they haue vniustly begun to demaunde of vs. For whosoeuer goeth about to defeate or dispossesse an other of his right, and to take from him that which is his owne; worthylie and deseruedlie may bee put from that, which is his owne, by him to whom he hath offered and done such wrong and violence. Seeing therefore, the Romaines would so gladly take from vs, that which is our owne, we will without doubt, take from them that, which they haue, if we may once come to buckle with them. Behold this is the conflict that al true hearted Britaines so long haue wished for: Behold these be the Prophesies of Sybilla now fulfilled, which so plainly and truely foretolde, that of the third stock of the Britaines there should one be borne, that should obtaine and possesse the Romain Empyre. Now, for two of these, the Prophesies bee alreadie fulfilled: sithence it is manifest (as thou hast alreadie declared) that those two most noble and excellent Princes Belinus and Constantine, ouercame, and gaue the Armes of the Romaine Empyre. And now haue we you, being the third, vnto whom such high exployt and honour is promised. Make haste therefore to receiue that which God is readie to bestowe on thee. Hasten (I say) to subdue that which he is willing should be subdued. Hasten to aduaunce all vs, that are here readie for thyne aduauncement & honour, neither to refuse woundes, nor to lose life and limme. And for thy better attchieuing hereof, I my selfe will accompanie thee with tenne thousand well armed Souldiours.

ANgusell King of Albania, when Howell had made an ende of his Oration, began to declare his lyking and opinion of the matter, in this sort following. Since the tyme that I heard my Lord vtter his mynd, touching this case, I haue conceiued such inwarde ioye as I am not able here afore you to expresse. For, in all our victorious Conquests alreadie passed, and in so many Kings and Regions as wee haue subdued, wee may well seeme to haue done nothing at all; if wee suffer the Romaines

and

.of VVales.

and Germaines still to remaine, and doe not manfully wrecke vpon them, those bloodie slaughters, which heretofore they inflicted vpon our Auncestors and Countreymen. And now sith wee haue occasion and libertie to trye the matter with them by force of armes, I reioyce exceedingly, and haue a longing thirst to see that day, wherein we may meete together; yea I thirst, euen as if I had bene drye and kept three daies, thirtie, from a Fountaine of water. Oh that I might see that day; how sweete and pleasant should those wounds be, that I should either giue or take, when we coape together! yea, death it self shall be sweete and welcome, so that I may suffer the same in reuenging our fathers, in defending our libertie, and in aduauncing our King. Let vs therefore giue the charge and onset vpon ponder effeminate and ineyrocke people, and let vs stand to our tackle like men: that after we haue banquished them, we may enioye their honors and offices with ioyfull victorie. And for my parte, I will augment our Armie with two thousand Horsemen well appoynted and armed, beside Footemen.

The sentence and resolution of the King of Albania.

FINIS.

Here followeth the Latin of the English going before.

OMnibus in vrbe legionum congregatio solemnitate instante Archipræsules Londinensis Eboracensis: necnon in vrbe legionum Archiepiscopus Dubricius ad pallatium ducuntur vt regem Arthurum diademate regali coronarent Dubricius ergo quoniam in sua ducoesi curia tenebatur: paratus ad celebrandum huius rei curam suscepit. Rege tandem insignito ad templum metropolitanæ sedis ornate conducitur: à dextro & à leuolatere duo Archipontifices ipsum tenebant. Quatuor autem reges viz. Anguselus rex Albaniæ, Caduallus Venedociæ rex, Cador rex Cornubiæ, & Sater rex Demetiæ: quatuor aureos gladios ante ipsum ferentes præibant. Conuentus quòque multimodo cum ordinatorum miris modulationibus præcinebat. Ex alia parte, reginam suis insignibus laureatam Archipræsules

E 3   atque

atque pontifices ad templum dicatarum puellarum condu-
cebant. Quatuor quoque prædictorum regum reginæ quatuor albas columbas de more præferebant.

Ecce enim duodecim viri maturæ etatis reuerendi vultus
ramos oliuæ in signum legationis in dextris ferentes mode-
ratis paſsibus ad regem ingrediuntur: & eo ſalutato literæ
ipſi ex parte Lucij Tiberij in hæc verba obtulerunt.

Lucij Romani Procuratoris ad Arthurum
Britonum regem epiſtola.

LVcius reipublicæ procurator Arthuro regi Britâniæ quid
meruit. Admirans vehementer admiror ſuper tuæ tyran-
nidis proternia. Admiror inquam & iniuriam quam Romæ
intuliſti recolligens, indignor quod extra te egreſſus eam
cognoſcere diffugias: nec animaduertere feſtines quid ſit
iniuſtis actibus ſenatum offendiſſe: cui totum orbem famu-
latum debere non ignoras. Etenim tributû Britanniæ quod
tibi ſenatus reddere precæperat: quia Caius Iulius ceteriq;
romanæ dignitatis viri illud multis temporibus habuerunt:
neglecto tanti ordinis imperio detinere præſumpſiſti. Eripuiſti quoque illi Galliam:eripuiſti Allobrogum prouinciâ:
eripuiſti omnes oceani inſulas: quarum reges dum romana
poteſtas in illis partibus perualuit, vectigal maioribus noſtris reddiderût. Quia ergo de tantis iniuriarum tuarum cu-
mulis ſenatus reparationem petere decreuit mediantê Au-
guſtum proximi anni terminum perfigens Romani te veni-
re iubeo:vt dominis tuis ſatisfaciens ſententie quam eorum
dictatori iuſticia acquieſcas. Sin aliter ipſe partes tuas adibo
& quicquid veſania tua reipublicæ erripuit eidem medianti-
bus gladijs reſtituere conabor.

Cadoris ducis Cornubiæ ad regem.

HVcuſq; in timore fueram ne Britones longa pace quietos
ocium quod ducunt ignauos faceret, famamque militiæ
qua

qua ceteris gentibus clariores cenfentur in eis omnino de-
leret. Quippe vbi vfus armorum videtur abeffe, alearum vero & mulierum inflamationes, ceteraque oblectamenta ad-
effe: dubitandum non eft quin quod erat virtutis: quod honoris, quod audaciæ: quod famæ ignauia commaculet. Fere
namque tranfacti funt quinque anni ex quo (predictis deli-
tijs dediti)exercitio Martis caruimus. Deus igitur vt nos feg-
nitia liberaret: Romanos in hunc affectum induxit vt in pri-
ftinum ftatum noftram probitatem reducerent . Hæc & hijs
fimilia illo cum cæteris dicente venerunt tandem ad fedilia
vbi collocatis fingulis: Arthurus illos in hunc modum affa-
tus.

Oratio Arthuri ad fuos.

COnfocij(inquit)aduerfitatis & profperitatis: quorum
probitatis hactenus, & in dandis cófilijs, & in militijs
agendis expertus fum : adhibete & monete nunc vn-
animiter fenfus veftros,& fapienter prouidete quæ fuper ta-
libus mandatis nobis effe agenda noueritis. Quicquid enim
à fapiente diligenter prouidetur cum ad actum accedit facilius toleratnr . Facilius ergo inquietationem Lucij tolerare
poterimus fi communi ftudio premeditati fuerimus quibus mofiis eam debilitare inftaremus . Quam non multum
timendam nobis effe exiftimo: cum ex irrationabili caufa
exigat tributum quod ex Britannia habere defiderat . Dicit
enim ipfum fibi dare debere quia Julio Cæfari ceterifque
fuccefforibus fuis redditum fuerit: qui difsidio prifcorū Britonum inuitatem cum armata manu in Britaniam applicue-
runt: atque patriam domefticis motibus vacillanté fuæ po-
teftati vi, & violétia fubmiferunt: Quia vero hoc modo eam
adepti fuerunt vectigal ex ea iniufte ceperunt. Nihil enim
quod vi vt violentia acquiritur iufte ab ipfo pofsidetur qui
violentiam metuit.

Irrationabilem ergo caufam pretendit : qua nos iure fibi
tributarios effe arbitratur . Quoniam ergo id quod iniuftū
eft

eſt à nobis præſumit exigere : conſimili ratione petamus ab
iſto tributum Romæ : & qui fortior ſuperuenerit ferat quod
habere exoptauit . Nam ſi quia Cæſar cæterique romani re-
gès Britanniam olim ſubiugauerunt vectigal nunc debere ſi-
bi ex illa reddi decernit : Similiter nunc ego cenſeo quam
Roma mihi tributum reddere debet: quia anteceſſores mei
eam antiquitus obtinuerunt. Belinus etenim ille Britonum
ſereniſsimus rex vſus auxilio fratris ſui, Brenni videlicet ducis Allobrogum : ſuſpenſis in medio foro viginti nobiliori-
bus Romanis:vrbem ceperūt, captámque multis temporibus poſſederunt . Conſtantinus etiam Helenæ filius necnon
& Maximianus vterque mihi cognatione propinquus alter
poſt alterum diademate Britanniç inſignitus:thronum Romani imperij adeptus eſt.Cenſetis ne ergo vectigal romanis
petendum ? De Gallia autem ſiue de collateralibus inſulis
oceani non eſt reſpondendum : cum illas diffugerent quando eaſdem poteſtati eorum ſubtrahebamus.

Hoeli regis minoris Bri-
tanniæ,reſponſio.

L Icet vnuſquiſque veſtrum totus in ſe reuerſus,omnia , &
omnibus animo tractare valuerit non exiſtimo eum præ-
ſtantius conſiliū poſſe inuenire quam iſtud quod modo diſ-
cretio ſolertis prudentiæ tuæ recoluit. Proinde etenim pro-
uidit nobis tua deliberatio Tulliano liquore lita. Vnde con-
ſtantis viri affectum : ſapientis animi effectum optimi con-
ſilij profectum laudare indeſinenter debemus. Nam ſi iuxta
prædictā rationem Romam adire volueris non dubito quin
triumpho potiamur : dum libertatem noſtrā tueamur dum
iuſte ab innimicis noſtris exigamus quod à nobis iniuſte petere incæperunt.Quicunque enim ſua alteri eripere conatur
merito quæ ſua ſunt per eum quem impetit amittit . Quia
ergo Romani noſtra nobis demere affectant:ſua illis procul
dubio: auferemus ſi authoritas nobis congrediendi præſta-

bitur . En congreſſus cunctis Britonibus deſiderandus . En Vaticinia Si-
bille de Brito-
nibus.
vaticinia ſibyllæ quæ veris angurijs teſtantur: ex Britannico
genere tertio naſciturum qui Romanum obtinebit imperiū.
De duobus autem adimpleta ſunt oracula: cum manifeſtum
ſit præclaros vt dixiſti principes Belinum atque Conſtanti-
num imperij Romani geſsiſſe inſignia & imperia . Nunc ve-
rò te tertium habemus, cui tātum culmen honoris promit-
titur . Feſtina ergo recipere : quod deus non differt largiri.
Feſtina ſubingare quod vltro vult ſubingari. Feſtina nos om- Exhortatio
Hoeli.
nes exaltare qui vt exalteris nec vulnera recipere: nec vitam
amittere diffugiamus . Vt autem hæc perficias decem milli-
bus armatorum præſentiam tuam conabor.,

ANguſelus Albaniæ rex: vt Hoelus finem dicendi fecerat:
quod ſuper hac re affectabat in huc modum manifeſtare
perrexit. Ex dominum meum ea quæ dixit affectare conieci:
tanta lætitia animo meo illapſa eſt : quantam nequeo in ve- Sententia regis
Albaniæ.
ſtra preſentia exprimere. Nihil enim in tranſactis debellati-
onibus quas tot & tantis regibus intulimus egiſſe videmur:
ſi Romani & Germani illeſi permaneant: nec in illos clades
quas olim noſtratibus ingeſſerunt viriliter vindicemus . Ac
nunc quoniam licentia congrediendi permittitur gaudens
admodū gaudeo & deſiderio diei quo conueniamus æſtuans
ſitio cruorem illorum quemadmodū fontem ſi triduo pro-
hiberer . O ſi illam lucem videbo quæ dulcia erunt vulnera
quæ vel recipiam vel inferam: quando dextras conferemus.
Ipſa etiam mors dulcis erit : dum eam in vindicando patres
noſtros: in tuendo libertatem noſtram: in exaltando regem
noſtrum perpeſſus fuero. Aggrediamur ergo ſemiuiros illos
& aggrediendo perſtemus vt deuictis ipſis eorum honoribus
cum læta potiamur victoria. Exercitum autem noſtrum duobus milibus armatorū equitum exceptis peditibus angebo.

FINIS.

Would to God we had the like aide of Kings and offer now
to daunt the pride of the Romish practiſes.

The worthines
The true Authors of this
whole Booke.

Iohannes Badius Afcenciu.
Merlinus Ambrofius.
Gualterus Monemotenfis.
Giraldus Cambrenfis.
Iohannes Bale of Brutus.
Ieffrey of Monmouth.
Gildas Cambrius, a Poet of Britaine.
Sibilla.

Annalles fue
gentes.

Two Brethren that were Martyrs, Iulius and Aron in Carleon, in whofe names two Churches were built there.

Thelians Epifcopus Landaph.

Saint Auguftine could not make the Britaines be obedient to the Archbifhop of Canterburie, but yet they onely fubmitted themfelues to the Archbifhop of Carleon, in Adelbrights tyme that was King of Kent.

A Hill moft
notable neere
Carleõ a myle
frõ the towne.

NOw muft I touch, a matter fit to knowe,
A Fort and ftrength, that ftands beyond this Towne:
On which you fhall, behold the nobleft fhowe,
(Looke round about, and fo looke rightly downe)
That euer yet, I fawe or man may view:
Upon that Hill, there fhall appeare to you,
Of feauen Shieres, a part and portion great,
Where Hill it felfe, is fure a warlike Seate.

Ten thoufand men, may lodge them there vnfeene,
In trebble Dykes, that gards the Fortreffe well:
And yet amid, the Fort a goodly gréene,
Where that a power, and mightie Campe may dwell:

J4

In spyte of world, if Soldiours victuall haue.
The Hill so stands, if Bird but wing doe waue,
Or man or beast, but once stirre vp the head
A Bowe aboue, with shaft shall strike it dead.

The Hill commaundes, a maruels way and scope,
It seemes it good, farre off for Townes defence,
And in the warres, it was Carleons hope:
Or els in deede, the Duke of Gloster sence
(That did destroy, both Towne and all therein)
To serue his turne, this Fortresse did begin.
Not farre from this, much like vnto the same,
Tombarlowm stands, a Mountaine of some fame.

A Towne nere this, that buylt is all a length,
Cal'd Neawport now, there is full fayre to viewe:
Which Seate doth stand, for profite more then strength,
A right strong Bridge, is there of Timber newe:
A Riuer runnes, full nere the Castle wall:
Nere Church likewise, a Mount behold you shall,
Where Sea and Land, to sight so plaine appeeres,
That there men see, a part of fiue fayre Sheeres.

As vpward hye, aloft to Mountaine top,
This Market towne, is buylt in healthfull sort:
So downeward loe, is many a Marchants shop,
And many sayle, to Bristowe from that Port.
Of auncient tyme, a Citie hath it bin,
And in those daies, the Castle hard to win:
Which yet shewes fayre, and is repayrd a parte,
As things decayd, must neeeds be helpt by arte.

A goodly Seate, a Tower, a princely pyle,
Built as a watch, or saftie for the Soyle,
By Riuer stands, from Neawport not three myle.
This house was made, when many a bloodie broyle,

A very high Hill of a maruellous strength which was a strong Fort in Arthurs daies.

Bellinus Magnus made this called Bellingstocke.

A wonderfull high mountaine with the like maner of defence.

The towne of Neawport.

On a round hill by the Church there is for Sea and Land the most princely sight that any man liuing at one instant may with perfect eye behold. The Towne hath Marchants in it. A Castle is at the end of this Towne, and full by the Bridges and Riuer. Greenefield Castle that was the Duke of Lancasters.

f 2

In

Eboyth is the Riuers name that runneth here.

In Wales God wot, destroyd that publicke state:
Here men with sword, and shield did brawles debate:
Here saftie stood, for many things in déede,
That sought sauegard, and did some sucker néede.

For Riuer, wood, pasture ayre, walke & pleasure, this place passeth.

The name thereof, the nature shewes a right,
Greenefield it is, full gay and goodly sure:
A fine sweete Soyle, most pleasant vnto sight,
That for delight, and wholesome ayre so pure,
It may be praisde, a plot sought out so well,
As though a King, should say here will I dwell:
The Pastures gréene, the woods, and water chére,
Sayth any Prince may buyld a Pallace héere.

A true iudgement of the commodities in Wales if the people there would be laborous.

And in this place, and many parts about,
Is grasse and Corue, and fertile ground enough:
And now a while, to speake of Wales throughout,
Where if men would, take paynes to plye the Plough:
Digge out of drosse, the treasure of the earth,
And fall to toyle, and labour from their birth:
They should as soone, to store of wealth attaine,
As other Soyles, whose people takes great paine.

Rychill

But most of Wales, likes better ease and rest,
(Loues meate and mirth, and harmelesse quiet daies)
Than for to toyle, and trouble brayne and brest,
To vere the mynd, with worldly wearie waies.
Some stand content, with that which God shall send,
And on their lands, their stock and store doth spend:
And rubs out life, cleane voyde of further care,
Because in worlld, right well to liue they are.

Yet were they bent, to proule and purchace still,
And search out wealth, as other Nations doe:
They haue a Soyle, a Countrey rich at will,
Which can them make, full quickly wealthie to.

They

of Wales.

They haue begun, of late to lime their land,
And plowes the ground, where sturdie Okes did stand:
Conuerts the meares, and marrish euery where,
Whose barraine earth, begins good fruite to beare.

They teare vp Trées, and takes the rootes away,
Makes stonie fieldes, smooth fertile fallowe ground:
Brings Pastures bare, to beare good grasse for Hay,
By which at length, in wealth they will abound.
Wales is this day (behold throughout the Shéeres,
In better state, than twas these hundred péeres:
More rich, more fine, and further more to tell,
Fewe men haue knowne, the Countrey halfe so well.

Whereas at first, they sought for Corne farre off,
(To helpe the wants, of Wales when grayne was deere)
Now on the boord, they haue both Chéese and lofe,
To shewe the world, in houft is greater cheere.
The open Plaine, that hath his rubbish lost,
Saith plentie is, through Wales in euery coast:
The well wrought ground, that thousands may behold,
Where thornes did growe, sayth now there springs vp gold.

I meane where weedes, and thistles long hath growne,
(Wild drosse and docks, and stinking nettles vile)
There Barley swéete, and goodly Wheate is sowne,
Which makes men rich, that liu'd in lacke long while.
No gift nor gayne, more great and good to man,
Then that which toyle, and honest labour wan:
What sweat of browes, brings in is sugred swéete,
Makes glad the mynd, and comforts hart and spréete.

The people of wales in many places thriues by labour day-lie, and gets great gayne through tillage.

I haue knowen many places so barraine, that they haue sought for corne farre of, who now are able to liue without helpe of any other Countrey.

F 3   Abor

Aborgaynies Towne is walled
round about, and hath fayre Suburbs alſo.

REturne I muſt, to my diſcourſe befoꝛe,
Of Boꝛꝛow townes, and Caſtles as they are:
Aborgaynie, behind I kept in ſtoꝛe,
Whoſe Seate and Soyle, with beſt may well compare.
The Towne ſomewhat, on ſtæpe and mounting hill,
With Paſtoꝛ grounds, and Medaowes great at will:
On euery ſide, huge Mountaines hard and hye,
And ſome thicke woods, to pleaſe the gazers eye.

It ſtands ouer two little Riuers, called Ceybbie and Ceyuennie, of which Ceyuẽnie, Aborgeuenie tooke the name.

The Riuer Oske, along the Uale doth paſſe,
Right vnderneath, an auncient Bꝛidge of ſtone:
A goodly woꝛke, when firſt it reared was,
(And yet the Shiere, can ſhewe no ſuch a one)
Makes men to knowe, old Buildings were not bare,
And newe things bluſh, that ſteps not ſo in place,
With ſuretie good, and ſhewe to ſtep on ſtage,
To make newe woꝛld, to honoꝛ foꝛmer age.

The Bridge of ſtone a eleuen fayre arches, and a great bridge of ſtone to come drylie to that bridge.

Foꝛ foꝛmer tyme, built Townes and Caſtles trim,
Made Bꝛidges bꝛaue, and ſtrong foꝛ tyme to come:
And our young daies, that doth in gloꝛie ſwim,
Holds hard in hand, that finger faſt may thome.
Looke what tyme paſt, made gallant freſh and fayꝛe,
Tyme preſent ſpoyles, oꝛ will not well repayꝛe:
As in this Towne, a ſtately Caſtle ſhoes,
Which loe to ruyne, and wꝛetched wꝛacke it goes.

Of the bountie of tyme paſt, and the hardnes of our age.

A fayꝛe and noble Caſtle belonging to the auncient houſe and race of the honoꝛable, the Lord of Aborgaynie

Moſt goodly Towers, are bare and naked laſt,
That cou'red were, with timber and good lead:
Theſe Towers p   and, as ſtreight as doth a ſhaft,
The walles whereb., might ſerue to ſome good ſteed.

# of Wales.

For found and thicke, and wondrous high withall,
They are in deede, and likely not to fall:
Would God therefore, the owner of the fame,
Did ftay them vp, for to encreafe his fame.

Who doth delight, to fee a goodly Plaine,
Faire Riuers runne, great woods and mountaines hye:
Let him a while, in any Tower remaine,
And he fhall fee, that may content the eye.
Great ruth to let, fo trim a Seate goe downe,
The Countries ftrength, and beautie of the Towne:
A Lordly place, a princely plot and viewe,
That laughs to fcorne, our patched buildings newe.

The bountie
of the Caftle
and Countrie.

The fhell of this, I meane the walles without,
The worthie worke, that is fo finely wrought:
The Sellers deepe, and buildings round about,
The firme Freeftone, that was fo derely bought;
Makes men lament, the loffe of fuch a thing,
That was of late, a houfe for any King.
Yea who fo wayes, the worth of Caftle yet,
With heauie mynd, in mufe and dump fhall fit.

A goodly and
ftately peece of
worke as like
to fall as be re-
payred againe.

To fee fo ftrong, and ftately worke decay,
The fame difeafe, hath Oske in Caftle wall:
Which on maine Rocke, was builded euery way,
And now God wot, is readie downe to fall.
A number more, in Monmouth Shiere I finde,
That can not well, abyde a blaft of winde:
The loffe is theirs, that fees them ouerthrowne,
The gaine were ours, if yet they were our owne.

Any heart in
the world
would pittie
the decay of
Caftles in Mō-
mouth fhiere.

Though Caftle here, through trackt of tyme is worne,
A Church remaines, that worthie is of note:
Where worthie men, that hath bene nobly borne,
Were layd in Tombe, which els had bene forgot.

In this church
was a moft
famous worke
in maner of a
genealogie of

And

Kings, called the roote of Iesse, which worke is defaced and pulled downe in peeces.

And buried cleane, in graue past mynd of man,
As thousand are, forgot since world began:
Whose race was great, and who for want of Tome,
In dust doth dwell, vnknowne till day of Dome.

On the right hand in a faire Chappell.

In Church there lyes a noble Knight,
Enclosde in wall right well:
Crosselegged as it seemes to sight,
(Or as recerd doth tell)

Both the windowe and in other parts about him shewes that he was a stranger.

He was of high and princely blood,
His Armes doth shewe the same:
For thereby may be vnderstood,
He was a man of fame.
A Shield of blacke he beares on brest,
A white Crowe plaine thereon:
A ragged sleeue in top and crest,
All wrought in goodly stone.

Blewe is.

The labell whereon are nyne Flowerdeluces.

And vnder feete, a Greyhound lyes,
Three golden Lyons gay,
Nine Flowerdeluces there likewise,
His Armes doth full display.

On the left hand a Lord of Aborgany.

A Lord that once enioyde that Seate,
Lyes there in sumptuous sort:
They say as loe his race was great,
So auncient men report.
His force was much: for he by strength
With Bull did struggle so,
He broke cleane off his hornes at length,
And therewith let him go.
This Lord a Bull hath vnder feete,
And as it may be thought,
A Dragon vnder head doth lye,
In stone full finely wrought.
The worke and Tombe so auncient is,
(And of the oldest guyse)

My

# of Wales.

My first bare view, full well may mis,
To shewe how well he lyes.

A Tombe in déede, of charge and showe,
Amid the Chappell stands:
Where William Thomas Knight ye knowe,
Lyes long with stretched hands.
A Harbert was he cal'd of right,
Who from great kindred cam,
And married to a worthie wight,
Daughter to Dauie Gam,
(A Knight likewise, of right and name)
This Harbert and his Féere,
Lyes there like one that purchast fame,
As plainly doth appéere.
His Tombe is rich, and rare to viewe,
Well wrought of great deuice:
Though it be old, Tombes made but newe,
Are of no greater price.
His Armes thrée ramping Lyons white,
Behind his head in shield:
A crowned Lyon blacke is hers,
Set out in most rich field:
Behind her head is likewise there,
Loe what our elders did,
To make those famous euery where,
Whose vertues are not hid.

In Tombe as trim as that before,
Sir Richard Harbert lyes:
He was at Banbrie field of yore,
And through the battaile twise:
He past with Pollax in his hands,
A manly act in déede,
To preace among so many bands,
As you of him may reede.

(marginal notes, right column)

Sir William Thomas Knight (alias) Harbert.

Sir Dauie Gam Knight father to this Knights wife.

This Knight was slaine at Edgingcourt field.

His Tombe is of hard and good Allablaster.

Sir William Thomas was father to the next that followes, called Sir Richard Harbert of Colbroke Knight.

In the Chronicle this is rehearsed.

This

The worthines

This valiant Knight, at Colbroke dwelt,
Nere Aborgaynie towne:
Who when his fatall destnie felt,
And Fortune flong him downe,
Among his enemies lost his head,
A rufull tale to tell:
Yet buryed was as I haue said,
In sumptuous Tombe full well.

On the left hand of the Chappell they lye.

His wife Dame Margret by his side,
Lyes there likewise for troth:
Their Armes as yet may be tryed,
(In honor of them both)
Stands at their heads, three Lyons white
He giues as well he might:
Three Rauens blacke, in shield she giues,
As Daughter to a Knight.
A sheafe of Arrowes vnder head,
He hath as due to him:
Thus there these worthie couple lye,
In Tombe full fine and trim.

She was daughter to Thomas ap Griffith father to Sir Rice ap Thomas Knight.

Now in another passing Tombe,
Of beautie and of charge,
There lyes a Squire(that Harbert hight)
With cost set out at large.
Two Daughters and sixe Sounes also,
Are there set nobly forth:
With other workes that makes the showe,
And Monument more worth.
Himselfe, his wife, and children to,
Lyes shrowded in that Seate:
Now somewhat for that Squire I do,
Because his race was great.

On the right hand of the Chappell.

He was the father of that Earle,
That dyed Lord Steward late,
A man of might, of spret most rare,

The old Earle of Penbroke one of the priuie Councell.

Ant

And bozne to happie fate.
His father layd so richly here,
So long agoe withall,
Shewes to the lokers on full cleere,
(When this to mynd they call)
This Squire was of an auncient race,
And bozne of noble blod:
Sith that he dyed in such a cace,
And left such wozdly god,
To make a Tombe so rich and bzaue:
Nay further now to say,
The thzée white Lyons that he gaue
In Armes, doth race bewzay:
And makes them blush and hold downe bzowe,
That babble out of square.
Rest there and to my matter now:
Upon this Tombe there are
Thzee Lyons and thzee white Bozes heads:
The first thzée are his owne.
The white Bozes heads his wife she gaue,
As well in Wales is knowne.
A Lyon at his feete doth lye,
At head a Dzagon gréene:
Moze things who lists to search with eye,
On Tombe may well be seene.

Amid the Church, Lozd Hastings lay,
Lozd Aborgaynie than:
And since his death remou'd away,
By fine deuice of man:
And layd within a windowe right,
Full flat on stonie wall:
Where now he doth in open sight,
Remaine to people all.
The windowe is well made and wzought,
A costly wozke to see:

In the windowe now be lyea.

G 2   In

In which his noble Armes are thought,
Of purpose there to bee.
A ragged sleeue and sire red Birds,
Is portrayd in the Glasse:
His wife hath there her left arme bare,
It seemes her sleeue it was
That hangs about his necke full fine,
Right ore a Purple wæde:
A robe of that same colour too,
The Ladie weares in deede.
Under his legges a Lyon red,
His Armes are rare and ritch:
A Harrold that could shewe them well,
Can blase not many sitch.
Sire Lyons white, the ground fayre blew,
Three Flowerdeluces gold:
The ground of them is red of hew,
And goodly to behold.
But note a greater matter now,
Upon his Tombe in stone

Some say this
great Lord
was called
Bruce and not
Haftings, but
most doe hold
opinion he
was called Ha-
ftings.

Were foretéene Lords that knées did bow,
Unto this Lord alone.
Of this rare worke a porch is made,
The Barrons there remaine
In good old stone, and auncient trade,
To shewe all ages plaine.
What homage was to Haftings due,
What honour he did win:
What Armes he gaue, and so to blaze
What Lord had Haftings bin.

A Ladie of A-
borgaynie.

Right ore againft this windowe, loe
In stone a Ladie lyes:
And in her hands a Hart I troe,
She holds before your eyes:
And on her breaft, a great fayre shield,

Iij

of Wales.

In which she beares no more
But three great Flowerdeluces large:
And euen loe, right ore
Her head another Ladie lyes
With Squirrell on her hand,
And at her feete, in stone likewise,
A couching Hound doth stand:
They say her Squirrell lept away,
And toward it she run:
And as from fall she sought to stay
The little pretie Bun,
Right downe from top of wall she fell,
And tooke her death thereby.
Thus what I heard, I doe you tell,
And what is seene with eye.

A Ladie of some noble house whose name I knowe not.

A friend of myne who lately dyed,
That Doctor Lewis hight:
Within that Church his Tombe Ilyyed,
Well wrought and fayre to sight.
O Lord (quoth I) we all must dye,
No lawe, nor learnings lore:
No iudgement deepe, nor knowledge hye,
No riches lesse or more,
No office, place, nor calling great,
No worldly pompe at all,
Can keepe vs from the mortall threat
Of death, when God doth call.
Sith none of these good gifts on earth,
Haue powre to make vs liue:
And no good fortune from our birth,
No power of breath can giue.
Thinke not on life and pleasure heere,
They passe like beames of Sunne:
For nought from hence we carrie cleere,
When man his race hath runne.

Doctor Lewis lately Iudge in the Amoraltie

The worthines
of An Introduction for
Breaknoke Shiere.

IS bodie tyerd with trauaile, God forbid,
That wearie bones, so soone should seeke for rest:
Shall sences sleepe, when head in house is hid,
As though some charme, were crept in quiet brest.
And so bewitch, the wits with too much ease,
That duls good spreete, and blunts quicke sharpe deuice:
Which climes the Clowdes, and wades through deepest Seas,
And goes before, and breakes the frozen Ice,
To cleere the coast, and make the passage free
For trau'lers all, that will great secrets see.

When quick conceyt, by slouth is rockt asleepe,
And fresh deuice, goes faynt for lacke of vse:
Along the limmes, doth lazie humours creepe,
And daylie breedes, in bodie great abuse.
If mettall fine, be not kept cleane from rust,
The brightest blade, will sure some cancker take:
And when cleere things, are staynd with drosse and dust,
They must be skour'd by skill, for profites sake.
Wit is nought worth, in ydle braine to rest,
Nor gold doth good, that still lyes lockt in chest.

The soft Downe bed, and Chamber warm'd with fire,
Or thicke furd gowne, is all that sluggard seekes:
But men of spreete, whose hearts do still aspire,
Do labour long, with leane and lentten checkes,
To trye the world, and taste both sweete and sower:
Who much doth see, may much both speake and write:
Who little knowes, hath little wit or power
To winne the wise, or dwell in worlds delight.
Feare not to toyle, for he that sowes in paine,
Shall reape with ioye, for store good Corne againe.

In reachlesse youth, whiles fancie flewe with winde,
Féete could not stay, the bodie mou'd so fast:
For euery part, thereof did answer minde,
Till aged yéeres, sayd wanton daies were past.
If that be true, sound iudgement should be fraught
With grauer thoughts, and greater things of weight:
Sith sober sence, at lightnesse now hath laught,
Thy reason should, set crooked matters streight:
And newly frame, a forme of fine deuice,
That vertue may, bring knowledge most in price.

To treate of tyme, and make discourse of men,
And how the world, doth chop and chaunge estate,
Doth well become, an auncient writers pen:
If skill will serue, such secretes to debate.
If no, hold on the course thou hast begun,
To talke of Townes, and Castles as they are:
And looke thou doe, no toyle nor trauaile shun,
To set forth things, that be both straunge and rare:
If age doe droope, and can abide no toyle,
When thou comest home, yet set out some swéete Soyle.

Though ioynts waxe stiffe, and bodie heauie growes,
And backe bends downe, to earth where corps must lye:
And legges be lame, and gowte créepes in the toes,
Cold crampe, and cough, makes groning goast to crye.
When fits are past, if any rest be found,
Plye pen againe, for that shall purchase praise:
Yea though thou canst, not ride so great a ground,
As all ore Wales, in thyne old aged daies:
Forget no place, nor Soyle where thou hast bin,
With Breaknocke Shiere, than now this booke begin.

Shewe what thyne eyes, are witnesse of for troth,
And leaue the rest, to them that after liues:

When

The worthines

When man is cal'd, away to graue he goeth,
Death steales the life, that God and nature giues.
Thou hast no state, nor pattent here on earth,
But borrowed breath, the bodie beares about:
Death daylie waytes, on life from hower of birth,
And when he lists, he blowes thy candle out.
Then leaue some worke, in worlde before thou passe,
That friends may say, loe here a writer was.

My Muse thus sayd, and so she shranke aside,
As though some Spreet, a space had spoke to mee:
With that I had, a friend of myne espyde,
That stood farre of, behind a Lawrell tree.
For whom I cal'd, and told him in his eare
My Muses tale: but therewithall his eyes
Bedeaw'd his cheekes, with many a bitter teare,
For sorrowe great, that from his heart did rise.
Oh friend (quoth he) thy race I see so short,
Thou canst not liue, to make of Wales report.

For first behold, how age and thy mishap,
Agreed in one, to tread thee vnder foote:
Thou wast long since, flong out of Fortunes lap,
When youths gay blowmes, forsooke both braunch and roote,
And left weake age, as bare as barraine stocke.
That neither fruite, nor leaues will growe vpon:
Can feeble bones, abide the sturdie shocke
Of Fortunes force, when youthfull strength is gon:
And if good chaunce, in youth hath fled from thee,
Be sure in age, thou canst not happie bee.

Tis hap that must, maintaine thy cost and charge,
By some such meane, as great good turnes are gote:
Els walke or ride, abroade the world at large,
And yet great mynd, but makes old age to dote.

Thy

Thy trauaile paſt, ſhewes what may after fall,
Long iourneys bꝛeedes, diſeaſe and ſickneſſe oft:
Thou haſt not health, noꝛ wiſhed wealth at call,
That glads the heart, and makes men looke aloft.
No ſoꝛer ſnib, noꝛ nothing nips ſo néere,
As feele much want, yet ſhewe a merrie chéere.

My newfound friend, no ſooner this had ſayd,
(Which tryall knowes, both true and woꝛds of weight)
But that my mynd, from trauaile long was ſtayd,
Saue that I tooke, in hand a iourney ſtreight,
Tꝺ Breakenoke Towne, whoſe Seate once thꝛoughly pend,
(With ſome ſuch notes, as ſeaſon ſerues therefoꝛe)
There all the reſt, of tople ſhould make an end,
With aged limmes, might trauaile Wales no moꝛe.
Right ſoꝛie ſiue, I can no further go,
Content perfoꝛce, ſith hap will haue it ſo.

Some men beggin, to build a goodly Seate,
And frames a woꝛke, of Timber bigge and large:
Yet long befoꝛe, the woꝛkmanſhip be greate,
Another comes, and takes that plot in charge.
Men may not doe, no moꝛe then God permits,
The mynd it thinkes, great things to bꝛing to paſſe:
But common courſe, ſo ſoone oꝛecomes the wits,
In péeces lyes, mans ſtate like bꝛoken glaſſe.
We purpoſe much, but little powrr we finde,
With good ſucceſſe, to anſwer mightie minde.

Well, that diſcourſe, let goe as matter paſt,
To Breakenoke now, my pen and muſe are pꝛeſt:
And ſith that Soyle, and towne ſhalbe the laſt,
That here I meane, to touch of all the reſt,
In bꝛiefeſt ſoꝛt, it ſhalbe wꝛitten out:
Yet with ſuch woꝛds, as caries credit ſtill,

As

As other works, in world can breede no dout:
So this small peece, shall shewe my great good will,
That for farewell, to worthie Wales I make,
That followes here, before my leaue I take.

O Happie princely Soyle, my pen is farre to bace,
My muse but serues in sted of sople, to giue a Iewell grace:
My bare inuention cold, and barraine verses vaine,
When they thy glory should vnfold, they do thy Countrie staine.
Thy worth some worthie may, set out in golden lines,
And blaze ye same, w^t colors gay, whose glistring beautie shines.
My boldnesse was to great, to take the charge in hand,
With wasted wits the braines to beat, to write on such a Land:
Whose people may compare, in high'st degree of praise,
With any now aliue that are, or were in elders daies.
Thy Townes and Castles fayre, so brauely stands in deede,
They should their honour much apayre, if they my verses neede.
A writers rurall rime, doth hinder thy good name:
For verse but entertaines the tyme, with toyes y^t fancies frame,
With Tullies sugred tongue, or Virgils sharpe engine,
Thy rare renowne should still be rong, or sung in verse deuine.
A simple Poets pen, but blots white paper still,
And blurres the brute & praise of men, for want of cunning quill.
If Ouids skill I had, or could like Homer write,
Or Dant would make my muses glad, to please ye worlds delite,
Or Chawser lent me in these daies, some of his learned tales,
As Petrarke did his Lawra praise, so would I speake of Wales.
But all to late I craue, for knowledge wit and sence:
For looke what gifts ye Gods the gaue, they tooke the al fró héce,
And left vs nought but bookes, to stare and pore vpon,
On which perchance blind bayard lookes, whé sight is gó.
Our former age did floe, with grace and learned lore,
Then farre behind they come I troe, that striue to run before.
We must goe lagging on, as legges and limmes were lame,
And though long since ye gole was gon, & wit hath won ye game.

We ſhall haue roume to play, and tyme and place withall,
To loke, to reade, to write and ſay, what ſhall in fancie fall.
But woe is me the while, that ouerweenes in want,
When world may at my boldnes ſmile, to ſee my ſkill ſo ſcant.
Yet write in Countries praiſe, that I cannot ſet out,
And ſtands diſcurag'd many waies, to trauaile Wales about.
Yet take now well in worth, the works I haue begun,
I can no further thing ſet forth, my daies are almoſt dun:
As candle cleere doth burne, to ſocket in ſmall tyme, (pryme.
So age to earth muſt needes returne, when youth hath paſt his

Now Breakenoke ſhiere, as falleth to thy lot,
In place a peere, thou art not ſure forgot:
Nor written of ſo much as I deſire:
For ſickneſſe long, made bodie ſoule retyre
Unto the Towne where it was borne and bred,
And where perhaps, on turffe muſt lye my hed.
When labors all, ſhall reape a graue for reſt,
And ſilent death, ſhall quiet troubled breſt:
Then as I now, haue ſomewhat ſayd on thee,
So ſhall ſome friend, haue tyme to write on mee.
Whoſe reſtleſſe muſe, and wearie waking minde,
To pleaſure world, did oft great leaſure finde:
And who reioyſt, and toke a great delight,
For knowledge ſake, to ſtudie reade and write.

❧ The Towne and Church
of Breakenoke.

THE Towne is built, as in a pit it were,
By water ſide, all lapt about with hille
You may behold a ruinous Caſtle there,
Somewhat defaſte, the walles yet ſtandeth ſtill.
Small narrowe ſtreates, through all the Towne ye haue,
Yet in the ſame, are ſondrie houſes braue:

Maiſter Gams
dwelles here.

Well

Doctor Aw-
berie hath a
house here.

Well built without, yea trim and fayre within,
With sweete prospect, that shall your fauour win.

The Riuer Oske, and Hondie runnes thereby,
Fower Bridges good, of stone stands ore each streame:
The greatest Bridge, doth to the Colledge lye,
A free house once, where many a rotten beame
Hath bene of late, through age and trackt of tyme:
Which Bishop now, refourmes with stone and lyme.
Had it not bene, with charge repayrd in haste,
That house and Seate, had surely gon to waste.

Two Churches doth, belong vnto this Towne,
One stands on hill, where once a Priorie was:
Which chaung'd the name, when Abbyes were put downe,
But now the same, for Parrish Church doth passe.
Another place, for Morning prayer is,
Made long agoe, that standeth hard by this.
Built in this Church, a Tombe or two I finde,
That worthie is, in briefe to bring to minde.

The auncient
house of
Gams.

Three couple lyes, one ore the others head,
Along in Tombe, and all one race and lyuer
And to be plaine, two couple lyeth dead,
The third likewise, as destinie shall assyne,
Shall lye on top, right ore the other twaine:
Their pictures now, all readie there remaine,
In signe when God appoynts the terme and date,
All flesh and blood must yeeld to mortall fate.

These are in deede, the auncient race of Gams,
A house and blood, that long rich Armes doth giue:
And now in Wales, are many of their names,
That keepes great trayne, and doth full brauely liue.
The eldest Sonne, and chiefest of that race,
Doth beare in Armes, a ramping Lyon crownd,

Ar3

of Wales.

And three Speare heads, and three red Cocks in place,
A Dragons head, all greene therein is found:
And in his mouth, a red and bloodie hand,
All this and more, vpon the Tombe doth stand.

Three fayre boyes heads, and euery one of those
A Serpent hath close lapt about his necke:
A great white Burke, and as you may suppose,
Right ore the same, (which doth it trimly decke)
A crowne there is, that makes a goodly shoe,
A Lyon blacke, and three Bulles heads I troe:
Three Flowerdeluce, all fresh and white they were,
Two Swords, two Crownes, with fayre long crosse is there.

The Armes of the Gams.

Three Bats, whose wings were spreaded all at large,
And three white barres were in these Armes likewise:
Let Harrolds now, to whom belongs that charge,
Describe these things, for me this may suffise.
Yet further now, I forced am to goe,
Of seuerall men, some other Armes to shoe.
Within that Church, there lyes beneath the Quere,
Their persons two, whose names now shall ye heare.

In Tombe of stone, full fayre and finely wrought,
One Waters lyes, with wife fast by his side:
Of some great stocke, these couple may be thought,
As by their Armes, on Tombe may well be tride.
Full at his feete, a goodly Greyhound lyes,
And at his head there is before your eyes
Three Libbarts heads, three cups, two Eagles splayd,
A fayre red Crosse: and further to be sayd,

The Armes of one Waters.

A Lyon blacke, a Serpent fiercely made,
With taple wound vp: these Armes thus endeth so.
Crosse legg'd by him, as was the auncient trade,
Debreos lyes, in picture as I troe,

His name was Reynold De-breos.

H 3   Of

The worthines

Of most hard wood:which wood as diuers say
No worme can eate, nor tyme can weare away:
A couching Hound, as Harrolds thought full méete,
In wood likewise, lyes vnderneath his féete.

Just by the same, Meredith Thomas lyes,
Who had great grace, great wit and worship both,
And world him thought, both happie blest and wise,
A man that lou'd, good Justice faith and troth.
Right ore this Tombe, of stone, to his great fame,
Good store in déede of Latin verses are,
And euery verse, set forth in such good frame,
That truely doth his life and death declare.
This man was likt, for many graces good
That he possest, besides his birth and blood.

❧ Somewhat of some Ri-
uers and VVaters.

Glasseberies
Bridge is with-
in two myle of
Porthamwell.

O F other things, as farre as knowledge goes,
Now must I write, to furnish forth this booke:
Some Shieres doe part at Waters, trpall showes
There, who so list vpon the same to looke.
Dulace doth runne, along vnto the Hay,
So Hartford shiere, from Breakenoke parteth there.
Brennick Deelyes, Thlauenny as they say
At Tawllgath méetes, so into Wye they beare:
From Arthurs Hill, Tytarell runnes apace,
And into Oske and Breakenoke runnes his race.

Maister Ro-
bert Knowles
that maried
one of the
heires of the
Vaughhans
hath a fayre
house and a
Parke at Port-
hamwell.

Here Breakenoke Towne, there is a Mountaine hye,
Which shewes so huge, it is full hard to clime:
The Mountaine seemes so monstrous to the eye,
Yet thousands doe repayre to that sometime.

And

And they that stand, right on the top shal see
A wonder great, as people doe report:
Which common brute, and saying true may bee,
But since in deede, I did not there resort,
I write no more, then world will witnesse well:
Let them that please, of those straunge wonders tell.

What is set downe, I haue it surely seene,
As one that toyld and trauayld for the troth:
I will not say, such things are as I weene,
And frame a verse, as common voyces goeth.
Nor yet to please the humors of some men,
I list not stretch, nor racke my termes away:
My muse will not so farre abuse the pen.
That writer shall gayne any blot thereby:
So he haue thanke in vsing ydle quill,
He seekes no more for paines and great good will.

¶ Ludloe Towne, Church
and Castle.

THE Towne doth stand most part vpon an Hill,
   Built well and fayre, with streates both large and wide:
The houses such, where straungers lodge at will.
As long as there the Councell lists abide,
Both fine and cleane the streates are all throughout,
With Condits cleere, and wholesome water springs:
And who that lists to walke the Towne about,
Shall finde therein some rare and pleasant things:
But chiefly there the ayre so sweete you haue,
As in no place ye can no better craue.

The Market house, where Corne and Cates are sold,
Is couered ore, and kept in finest sort:

The names of
streates there.
Castle streate.
Broad streate.
Old streate.
And the Mill
streate.
A fayre house
by the gate of
the making of
Justice Walter.

From

The worthines

Here this is a fayre house of Maister Sack- fords which he did buyld, and a fayre houſe that Maiſter Secre- tarie Foxe did beſtowe great charges on, & a houſe that Maiſter Berrie dwelles in. Mr Townes- end hath a fayre houſe at Saint Auſtins once a Frierie. The Lord Pre- ſident Sir Har- rie Sidneys Daughter, cal- led Ambroſia, is entombed here in moſt braueſt maner and great chargeable workmanſhip on the right hand of the Aulter. On the ſame is my Lord of Warwicks Armes excel- lently wrought, and my Lord Preſidents Armes and o- thers, are in like ſort there richly ſet out.

From which ye ſhall, the Caſtle well behold,
And to which walke, doe many men reſort.
On euery ſide thereof fayre houſes are,
That makes a ſhewe, to pleaſe both mynd and eye:
The Church nere that, where monuments full rare
There is, (wherein doth ſondrie people lye)
My pen ſhall touch, becauſe the notes I finde
Therein, deſerue to be well boꝛne in minde.

Within the Quere, there is a Ladie layd
In Tombe moſt rich, the top of fayre Touchſtone:
There was beſtow'd in honour of this mayd,
Great coſt and charge, the trueth may well be knowne.
Foꝛ as the Tombe, is built in ſumptuous guiſe,
So to the ſame, a cloſet fayre is wꝛought,
Where Loꝛds may ſit in ſtately ſolemne wiſe,
As though it were a fine deuice of thought,
To beautifie both Tombe and euery part
Of that fayre woꝛke, that there is made by arte.

Againſt that Tombe, full on the other ſide,
A Knight doth lye, that Iuſtice Towneſend hight:
His wife likewiſe, ſo ſoone as that ſhe dyed,
In this rich Tombe, was buryed by this Knight:
And trueth to tell, Dame Alice was her name,
An Heire in deede, that bꝛought both wealth and land,
And as woꝛld ſayth, a woꝛthie vertuous Dame,
Whoſe auncient Armes, in colours there doth ſtand:
And many moꝛe, whoſe Armes I doe not knowe,
Unto this Knight, are ioyned all a roe.

Amid the Church, a Chantrie Chappell ſtands,
Where Hozier lyes, a man that did much good:
Beſtow'd great wealth, and gaue thereto ſome lands,
And helpt poꝛe ſoules that in neceſſitie ſtood.

Aij

# of Wales.

As many men, are bent to win good will
By some good turne, that they may freely showe:
So Hoziers hands, and head were working still:
For those he did, in det or daunger knowe.
He smyld to see, a begger at his doore:
For all his ioye, was to releeue the poore.

Another man, whose name was Cookes for troth,
Like Hozier was, in all good gifts of grace:
This Cookes did giue, great lands and liuings both,
For to maintaine, a Chauntrie in that place.
A yéerely dole, and monthly almes likewise
He ordayud there, which now the poore doe mis:
His wife and he, within that Chappell lyes,
Where yet full plaine, the Chauntrie standing is:
Some other things, of note there may you see
Within that Church, not touched now by mée.

Yet Beawpy must, be nam'd good reason why,
For he bestow'd, great charge before he dyde,
To helpe poore men, and now his bones doth lye
Full nere the Font, vpon the formost side.
Thus in those daies, the poore was lookt vnto,
The rich was glad, to fling great wealth away:
So that their almes, the poore some good might do.
In poore mens bore, who doth his treasure lay,
Shall finde againe, ten fold for one he leaues:
Or els my hope, and knowledge me deceiues.

THE Castle now, I mynd here to set out,
It stands right well, and pleasant to the vewe,
With sweete prospect, yea all the field about.
An auncient Seate, yet many buildings newe
Lord President made, to giue it greater fame:
But if I must, discourse of things as true,

I

There

Sir Robert Townes-end Knight lyes in a maruelos fayre Tombe in the Queere here, and his wife by him, at his feete is a red Rowbuck, and a word *tout en dieu.* On the left hand Hozier lyes in the bodie of the Church. On the righe hand Cookes lyes. This man was my mothers father. Beawpy was a great ritch and verteous man, he made another Chantrie.

The Castle of Ludloe.

Sir Harry Sidney built many things here worthie praise and memorie.

The worthines

There are great works, that now doth beare no name,
Which were of old, and yet may pleasure you
To see the same: for loe in elders daies
Was much bestow'd, that now is much to praise.

Over a Chimney excellently wrought in the best chamber, is S. Androwes Crosse ioyned to Prince Arthurs Armes in the hall windowe.
Prince Arthurs Armes, is there well wrought in stone,
(A worthie worke, that fewe or none may mend)
This worke not such, that it may passe alone:
For as the tyme, did alwaies people send
To world, that might exceede in wit and sprœte:
So sondrie sorts of works are in that Seate,
That for so hye a stately place is mœte:
Which shewes this day, the workmanship is greate.
Looke on my Lords, and speak your fancies throw,
And you will praise, fayre Ludloe Castle now.

In it besides, (the works are here vnnam'd)
A Chappell is, most trim and costly sure,
So brauely wrought, so fayre and finely fram'd,
That to worlds end, the beautie may endure.
About the same, are Armes in colours sitch,
As fewe can shewe, in any Soyle or place:
A great deuice, a worke most rare and ritch:
Which truely shewes, the Armes, the blood and race
Of sondrie Kings, but chiefly Noble men,
That here in prose, I will set out with pen.

All that followes are Armes of Princes and Noblemen.

Sir Walter Lacie was first owner of Ludloe Castle, whose Armes are there, and so followes the rest by order as you may reade.

Jeffrey Genvuile, did match with Lacie.

Roger Mortymer the first Earle of Martchy an Earle of a great house matcht with Genvuile.

Leonell

Leonell Duke of Clarence ioyned with Ulster in Armes.

Edmond Earle of Marchy matched with Clarence.

Richard Earle of Cambridge matcht with the Earle of Marchy.

Richard Duke of Yorke matcht with Westmerland.

Edward the fourth matcht with Wodule of Riuers.

Henry the seuenth matcht with Elizabeth right heire of England.

Henry the eight matcht with the Marquese of Penbroke.

These are the greatest first to be named that are there set out worthely as they were of dignitie and birth.

Now followes the rest of those that were Lord Presidents, and others whose Armes are in the same Chappell.

William Smith Bishop of Lincolne was the first Lord President of Wales in Prince Arthurs daies.

Ieffrey Blythe Bishoppe of Couentrie and Litchfield Lord President.

Rowland Leé Bishoppe of Couentrie and Litchfield Lord President.

Ihon Veslie Bishop of Exeter Lord President.

Richard Sampson Bishop of Couentrie and Litchfield Lord President.

John

The worthines

John Dudley Earle of Warwick (after Duke of Northumberland) Lord President.

Sir William Harbert (after Earle of Penbroke) Lord President.

Nicholas Heath Bishop of Worcester Lord President.

Sir William Harbert once againe Lord President.

Gilbert Browne Bishop of Bathe and Welles Lord President.

Lord Williams of Tame Lord President.

Sir Harrry Sidney Lord President.

Sir Andrew Corbret Knight, Uicepresident.

There are two blancks left without Armes.

Sir Thomas Dynam Knight, is mentioned there to doe some great god act.

John Scory Bishop of Hartford.

Nicholas Bullingham, Bishop of Worcester.

Nicholas Robinson, Bishop of Bangore.

Richard Dauies, Bishop of Saint Dauies.

Thomas Dauies, Bishop of Saint Assaph.

Sir Iames Crofts Knight, Controller,

Sir John Throgmorton Knight, Justice of Chester and the three Shieres of Eastwales.

Sir Hugh Cholmley Knight.

Sir Nicholas Arnold Knight.

Sir George Bromley Knight, and Justice of the three shieres in Wales.

William Gerrard, Lord Chauncellor of Ireland, and Justice of the three Shieres in Southwales.

Charles Fore Esquier and Secretorie.

Ellice Price Doctor of the Lawe.

Edward Leighton Esquier.

Richard Seborne Esquier.

Richard Pates Esquier.

Rafe Barton Esquier.

George Pherpplace Esquier.

William Leighton Esquier.

Myles Sauds Esquier.

The Armes of al these afore spoken of are gallantly and cunningly set out in the Chappell.

Now is to be rehearsed, that Sir Harry Sidney being Lord President, buylt twelue rounnes in the sayd Castle, which goodly buildings doth shewe a great beautie to the same.

The great water called Tea, comes 17. mile frō a place called the Whitehall neere vnto Begyldie in the County of Radnor.

J 3

He made alſo a goodly Wardrope vnderneath the new Par-
lor, and repayred an old Tower, called Mortymers Tower, to
kéepe the auncient Records in the ſame: and he repayred a fayre
roume vnder the Court houſe, to the ſame entent and purpoſe,
and made a great wall about the woodyard, & built a moſt braue
Condit within the inner Court: and all the newe buildings ouer
the Gate Sir Harry Sidney (in his daies and gouernement
there) made and ſet out to the honour of the Quéene, and gloꝛie
of the Caſtle.

The Forreſt of Brenwood is weſt from the towne.
The Chace of Mocktrie and Ockley Parkes ſtãds not farre from thence.

There are in a goodly oꝛ ſtately place ſet out my Loꝛd Earle
of Warwicks Armes, the Earle of Darbie, the Earle of Woꝛ-
ceſter, the Earle of Pembꝛoke, and Sir Harry Sidneys Armes
in like maner: al theſe ſtand on the left hand of the Chamber. On
the other ſide are the Armes of Noꝛthwales and Southwales,
two red Lyons and two golden Lyons, Pꝛince Arthurs.

A deuice of the Lord Pre-ſidents.

At the end of the dyning Chamber, there is a pꝛetie deuice
how the Hedgehog bꝛake the chayne, and came from Ireland to
Ludloe.

There is in the Hall a great grate of Iron of a huge height:
ſo much is wꝛitten only of the Caſtle.

The Towne of Ludloe, and many
good gifts graunted to the ſame.

He gaue great poſſeſſions, large liberties, and did incor-porate them with many goodly free-domes.

KIng Edward fourth, foꝛ ſeruice truely done,
When Henry ſirt, and he had moꝛtall warre:
No ſoner he, by foꝛce the victoꝛie wone,
But with great things, the Towne he did pꝛefarre.
Gaue lands thereto, and libertie full large,
Which royall gifts, his bountie did declare,
And dayly doth, mainteyne the Townes great charge:
Whoſe people now, in as great freedome are,

As any men, vnder this rule and Crowne,
That liues and dwels, in Citie or in Towne.

Two Bayliefes rules, one yeere the Towne throughout,
Twelue Aldermen, they haue there in likewise:
Who doth beare swap, as turne doth come about,
Who chosen are, by oth and auncient guise.
Good lawes they haue, and open place to pleade,
In ample sort, for right and Iustice sake:
A Preacher too, that dayly there doth reade,
A Schoolemaster, that doth good schollers make.
And for the Queere, are boyes brought vp to sing,
And so serue God, and doe none other thing.

Three tymes a day, in Church good Saruice is,
At sixe a clocke, at nine, and then at three:
In which one howers, a straunger shall not mis,
But sondrie sorts, of people there to see.
And thirtie three, poore persons they maintaine,
Who weekely haue, both money, almes and mde:
Their lodging free, and further to be plaine,
Still once a weeke, the poore are truely payde:
Which shewes great grace, and goodnesse in that Seate,
Where rich doth see, the poore shall want no meate.

An Hospitall, there hath benelong of old,
And many things, pertayning to the same:
A goodly Guyld, the Township did vphold,
Vp Edwards gift, a King of worthie fame.
This Towne doth choose, two Burgesses alwaies
For Parliament, the custome still is so:
Two Fayres a yeere, they haue on seuerall daies,
Three Markets kept, but monday chiefe I troe:
And two great Parkes, there are full neere the Towne,
But those of right, pertaine vnto the Crowne.

That Towne hath bin well gouerned a log while with two Bayliefes, twelue Aldermen, and fiue and thirtie Commoners, a Recorder & a Towneclarke assistant to the sayd Bayliefes by iudiciall course of lawe weekely, in as large and ample maner for their triall betweene partie and partie, as any Cittie or Borrowe of England hath.

The poore haue sweete lodgings each one a part to himselfe. An Hospitall called S. Iones. A Guyld that King Edward (by Letters Pattents) gaue to the Bayliefs and Burgesses of the towne. The Aldermē are Iustices of the Peace for the time being

These

The worthines

These things rehearst, makes Ludloe honord mitch,
And world to thinke, it is an auncient Seate:
Where many men, both worthie wise and ritch
Were borne and bred, and came to credit great.
Our auncient Kings, and Princes there did rest,
Where now full oft, the President dwels a space:
It stands for Wales, most apt, most fit and best,
And neerest to, at hand of any place:
Wherefore I thought, it good before I end,
Within this booke, this matter should be pend.

The rest of Townes, that in Shropshiere you haue,
I neede not touch, they are so throughly knowne:
And further more, I knowe they cannot craue
To be of Wales, how euer brute be blowne.
So wishing well, as duetie doth me binde,
To one and all, as farre as power may goe,
I knit vp here, as one that doth not minde
Of natiue Soyle, no further now to showe.
So cease my mule, let pen and paper pause,
Till thou art calde, to write of other cause.

❧ An Introduction to re-
member Shropshiere.

HOw hath thy muse so long bene luld a sleepe?
What deadly drinke, hath sence in slumber brought?
Doth poyson cold, through blood and bosome creepe?

A deuice of
the Author
called Reasons
threatning.

Or is of spite, some charme by witchcraft wrought,
That vitall sprcetes, hath lost their feeling quite?
Or is the hand, so weake it cannot write?
Come pole man, and shewe some honest cause,
Why writers pen, makes now so great a pause.

Full from Welchbridge, along by meddowes greene,
The Riuer runs, most fayre and fine to vewe:
Such fruitfull ground, as this is seldome seene
In many parts, if that I heare be true.
Yet each man knowes, that grasse is in his pride,
And ayre is fresh, by euery Riuers side:
But sure this plot, doth farre surpasse the rest,
That by good lot, is not with graces blest.

There is a bridge called Welshbridge, which shewes Shrewseburie to be of Wales

Who hath desire, to vewe both hill and vale,
Walke vp old wall, of Castle rude and bare,
And he shall see, such pleasure set to sale,
In kindly sort, as though some Marchants ware
Were set in shop, to please the passer by:
Or cis by shewe, beguyld the gazers eye:
For looke but downe, along the pleasant coast,
And he shall thinke, his labour is not lost.

The Castle though old and ruynate stands most braue and gallantly.

Maister Prince his house stads so trim and finely, that it graceth all the Soyle it is in.

One way appeares, Stonebridge and Subbarbs there,
Which called is, the Abbey Forehed yet:
A long great streate, well builded large and faire,
In as good ayre, as may be wisht with wit:
Where Abbey stands, and is such ring of Belles,
As is not found, from London vnto Welles:
The Steeple yet, a gracious pardon findes,
To bide all blasts, all wethers stormes and windes.

Another way, full ore Welshbridge there is,
An auncient streate, cal'd Franckwell many a day:
To Ozestri, the people passe through this,
And vnto Wales, it is the reddie way.
In Subbarbs to, is Castle Forehed both,
A streate well pau'd, two seuerall waies that goeth:
All this without, and all the Towne within,
When Castle stood, to vewe hath subiect bin.

Here is the way to Meluerley, to Wattels Borrow where Ma. Leighton dwelles, to Cawx Castle Lord Staffords, and to Maister Williams house.

But

The worthines

Aldermen in
Scarlet orderly
in Shrewſebu-
rie, and two
Baylieſes as
richly ſet out
as any Mayor
of ſome great
Cities.

But now doth hold, their fréedome of the Prince,
And as is found, in Records true vnfaynd,
This trim ſhiere towne, was buplt a great while ſince:
Whoſe priuiledge, by loyaltie was gaynd.
Two Baylieſes there, doth rule as courſe doth fall,
In ſtate like Maior, and orders good withall:
Each officer due, that ſits for ſtately place,
Each péere they haue, to yéeld the roume more grace.

Great & coſtly
banquetting
in Chriſtmas
and at all Seſ-
ſions & Sizes.

On ſollemne daies, in Scarlet gownes they goe,
God houſe they képe, as cauſe doth ſerue therefore:
But Chriſtmas feaſts, compares with all I knowe
Saue London ſure, whoſe ſtate is farre much more.
That Cities charge, makes ſtraungers bluſh to ſee,
So princely ſtill, it is in each degrée:
But though it beare, a Torch beyond the beſt,
This Lanterne light, may ſhine among the reſt.

A matter of
trafficke to be
noted and cō-
ſidered of.

London com-
pared to the
flowing Sea.

This Towne with more, ſit members for the head,
Makes London ritch, yet reapes great gayne from thence:
It giues good gold, for Clothes and markes of lead,
And for Welſh ware, exchaungeth Engliſh pence.
A fountaine head, that many Condits ſerue,
Képes moyſt drye Springs, and doth it ſelfe preſerue:
The flowing Sea, to which all Riuers run,
May ſpare ſome ſhewres, to quench the heate of Sun.

The great
muſt main-
taine the ſmal.

So London muſt, like mother to the Realme,
To all her babes, giue milke, giue ſucke and pap:
Small Brookes ſwelles vp, by force of mightie ſtreame,
As little things, from greateſt gaynes good hap.
If Shrewſebrie thriue, and laſt in this good lucke,
It is not like, to lacke of worldly mucke:
The trade is great, the Towne and Seate ſtands well,
Great health they haue, in ſuch ſwéete Soyles that dwell.

Thus

# of Wales.

Thus farre I goe, to proue this Wales in déede,
Or els at least, the martches of the same:
But further speake, of Shiere it is no néede,
Saue Ludloe now, a Towne of noble fame:
A goodly Seate, where oft the Councell lyes,
Where Monuments, are found in auncient guyse:
Where Kings and Quéenes, in pompe did long abyde,
And where God pleasde, that good Prince Arthur dyde.

*Ludloe is set
out after.*

This Towne doth front, on Wales as right as lyne,
So sondrie Townes, in Shropshiere doe for troth:
As Ozestry, a prettie Towne full fine,
Which may be lou'd, be likte and praysed both.
It stands so trim, and is maintaynd so cleane,
And péopled is, with folke that well doe meane:
That it deserues, to be enrould and shrynd
In each good breast, and euery manly mynd.

*Ozestrie and
Bishops Ca-
stle doth front
in Wales.*

The Market there, so farre excédes withall,
As no one Towne, comes néere it in some sort:
For looke what may, be wisht or had at call,
It is there found, as market men report.
For Poultrie, Foule, of euery kind somewhat,
No place can shewe, so much more cheape then that:
All kind of Cates, that Countrie can afford,
For money there, is bought with one bare word.

*Of a notable
market a mer-
uelous matter.*

They hacke not long, about the thing they sell,
For price is knowne, of each thing that is brought:
Poore folke God wot, in Towne no longer dwell,
Then money had, perhaps a thing of nought:
So trudge they home, both barelegge and vnshod,
With song in Welch, or els in praysing God:
O swéete content, O merrie mynd and mood,
With sweat of browes, thou lou'st to get thy food.

*Poore folkes
makes fewe
words in bar-
gayning.*

The worthines

The blessed-
nesse of plaine
people.

O plaine good folke, that haue no craftie braines,
O Conscience cleere, thou knowst no cunning knacks:
O harmlesse hearts, where feare of God remaines,
O simple Soules, as sweete as Uirgin waxe.
O happie heads, and labouring bodies blest,
O sillie Doues, of holy Abrahams brest:
You slæpe in peace, and rise in ioye and blisse,
For Heauen hence, for you prepared is.

A rare report
yet truely gi-
uen of Wales.

Where shall we finde, such dealing now adaies?
Where is such cheere, so cheape and chaunge of fare?
Ride North and South, and search all beaten waies,
From Barwick bounds, to Venice if you dare,
And finde the like, that I in Wales haue found,
And I shall be, your slaue and bondman bound.
If Wales be thus, as tryall well shall proue,
Take Wales goodwill, and giue them neighbours loue.

You must
reade further
before you
finde Ludloe
described.

To Ludloe now, my muse must needes returne,
A season short, no long discourse doth craue:
Tyme rouleth on, I doe but daylight burne,
And many things, in deede to doe I haue.
Looke what great Towne, doth front on Wales this hower,
I minde to touch, God sparing life and power:
Not hyerd thereto, but hal'de by harts desire
To giue them praise, whose deedes doe fame require.
Verte folium.

¶ Of Shrewsebury Churches and the Monuments
therein, with a Bridge of stone two bowshot long, and
a streate called Colam, being in the Subbarbs,
and a fayre Bridge there in like maner: all
this was forgotten in the first copie.

The Authors
forgetfulnesse
excused.

I had such haste, in hope to be but briefe,
That Monuments, in Churches were forgot:

And

# of VVales.

And somewhat more, behind the walles as chiefe,
Where Playes haue bin, which is most worthie note,
There is a ground, newe made Theator wise,
Both deepe and hye, in goodly auncient guise:
Where well may sit, ten thousand men at ease,
And yet the one, the other not displease.

A spare belowe, to bayt both Bull and Beare,
For Players too, great roume and place at will.
And in the same, a Cocke pit wondrous feare,
Besides where men, may wrastle in their fill.
A ground most apt, and they that sits aboue,
At once in vewe, all this may see for loue:
At Astons Play, who had beheld this then,
Might well haue seene, there twentie thousand men.

Fayre Seuarne streame, runs round about this ground,
Saue that one side, is closde with Shrewsebrie wall:
And Seuarne bankes, whose beautie doth abound,
In that same Soyle, behold at will ye shall.
Who comes to marke, and note what may be seene,
Shall surely see, great pleasures on this greene:
Who walkes the bankes, and thinkes his payne not greate,
Shall say the Towne, is sure a princely Seate.

Without the walles, as Subbarbs buylded bée,
So doe they stand, as armes and legges to Towne:
Each one a streate, doth answer in degrée,
And by some part, comes Seuarne running downe:
As though that streame, had mynd to garde them all,
And as through bridge, this flood doth dayly fall,
So of Freestone, thrice Bridges bigge there are,
All stately built, a thing full straunge and rare.

Then iudge by this, and other things a heape,
They had déepe skill, that first the founders were:

L   End

A pleasant
and artificiall
peece of groud

A Master Aston
was a good
and godly
Preacher.

A Friery house
stood by this
ground called
the Welsh
Fryers.
In Shrewsebu-
rie were three
Fryer houses.

The worthines

So right they should,the fruite of labour reape,
Whose wit and wealth,did all the charges beare.
O fathers wise,and wits beyond the nicke,
That had the head,the sprites and sence so quicke:
O golden age,that car'de not what was spent,
So leaden daies,did stand therewith content.

Gold were those peeres,that sparde such siluer pence,
And brazen world,was that which horded all:
The leaden daies,that we haue sauerd since,
Bytes to the bones,and tasteth worse then gall.
What newe things now,with franknesse well begun,
Can staine those deedes,our fathers old haue done:
Great Townes they buylt,great Churches reard likewise,
Which makes our fame,to fall and theirs to rise.

Loke on the works,and wits of former age,
And our tyme shall,come dragging farre behind:
If both tymes might,be plainly playd on stage,
And old tyme past,be truely calde to mind,
For all our braue,fine glorious buyldings gay,
Tyme past would run,with all the fame away.
Aske Oxford that,and Cambridge if it please,
In this one poynt,shall you resolue at ease.

A briefe dis-
course of aun-
cient tyme.

In aunciaent tyme,our elders had desire,
To buyld their Townes,on steepe and stately hill:
To shewe that as,their hearts did still aspyre,
So should their works,declare their worthie will.
And for that then,the world was full of strife,
And fewe men stod,assur'd of land or life:
Such quarrels rose,about great rule and state,
That no one Soyle,was free from foule debate.

The occasion
of building
strong Holds.

For which sharpe cause,that dayly bred discord,
They made strong Holds,and Castles of defence:

And

And such as weare, the Kings the Prince and Lord
Of any place, would spare for no expence,
To see that safe, that they had hardly won:
For which sure poynt, were Forts and Townes begun:
And further loe, if people waxed wyld,
They brought in feare, by this both man an child.

And if men may, iudge who had most ado,
Or gesse by Forts, and Holds what Land was best:
Or looke vpon, our common quarrels to:
Or search what made, men seeke for peace and rest,
Behold but Wales, and note the Castles there,
And you shall finde, no such works any where:
So old so strong, so costly and so hye,
Not vnder Sunne, is to be seene with eye.

Wales hath a wonderfull number of Castles.

And to be plaine, so many Holds they haue,
As sure it is, a world to marke them well:
Pause there a while, my muse must pardon craue,
Pen may not long, vpon such matter dwell.
Now Denbigh comes, to be set foorth in verse,
Which shall both Towne, and Castle here rehearse:
So that the verse, such credit may attayne,
As writer shall, not lose no péece of payne.

A description of Denbigh-shiere.

❧An Introduction to bring
in Denbighshiere.

Hath slouth and sleepe, bewitcht my sences so,
That head cannot, awake the pole hand:
Is frendly muse, become so great a foe,
That labring pen, in penner still shall stand.
What trifeling tape, doth trouble writers brayne,
That earnest loue, forgets swéete Poets vayne:

A conceyted toy to set a broach an earnest matter.

L 2   Bid

Bid welcome mirth, and sad conceytes adue,
And fall againe, to write some matter newe.

Let old deuice, a Lanterne be to this,
To giue skill light, and make sound iudgement see:
Since gazing eyes, hath seene what each thing is,
And that no Towne, nor Soyle is hid from thee:
Set forth in verse, as well this Countrey here,
As thou at large, hast set out Monmouthshiere:
Praise one alone, the rest will thee disdaine,
A day may come, at length to quite thy paine.

Being Muster-maister of Kent more chargeable then well cōsidered of there.

Though former toyles, be lost in Sommer last,
Dispayre not now, for Wales is thankfull still:
Thou hast gon farre, the greatest brunt is past,
Then forward passe, and plucke not backe goodwill,
Put hand to Plough, like man goe through with all,
Thy ground is good, run on thou canst not fall:
When seede is sowne, and tyme bestowes some paine,
Thou shalt be knowne, a reaper of good graine.

Hold on thy course, and trauaile Wales all ore,
And whet thy wits, to marke and note it well:
And thou shalt see, thou neuer saw'st before,
Right goodly things, in deede that doth excell:
More auncient Townes, more famous Castles old,
Then well farre of, with ease thou mayst behold:
With Denbighshiere, thy second worke begin,
And thou shalt see, what glorie thou shalt win.

Chirke Castle a goodly and princely house yet

So I tooke horse, and mounted vp in haste,
From Monmouthshiere, a long the coasts I ryde:
When frost and snowe, and waymard winters waste,
Did beate from tree, both leaues and Sommers pryde,
I entred first, at Chirke, right ore a Brooke,
Where staying still, on Countrey well to looke.

# of Wales.

A Castle fayre, appéerde to sight of eye,
Whose walles were great, and towers both large and hye.

Full vnderneath, the same doth Kéeryock run,
A raging Brooke, when rayne or snowe is greate:
It was some Prince, that first this house begun,
It shewes farre of, to be so braue a Seate.
On side of hill, it stands most trim to vewe,
An old strong place, a Castle nothing newe.
A goodly thing, a princely Pallace yet,
If all within, were throughly furnishe fit.

Beyond the same, there is a Bridge of stone,
That stands on Dée, a Riuer déepe and swift:
It seemes as it, would riue the Rocks alone,
Or vndermyne, with force the craggie Clift.
To Chester runs, this Riuer all along,
With gushing streame, and roring water strong:
On both the sides, are bankes and hilles good store,
And mightie stones, that makes the Riuer rore.

It flowes with winde, although no rayne there bée,
And swelles like Sea, with waues and foming floud:
A wonder sure, to see this Riuer Dée,
With winde alone, to waxe so wyld and wood,
Make such a sturre, as water would be mad,
And shewe such life, as though some spréete it had.
A cause there is, a nature for the same,
To bring this floud, in such straunge case and frame.

Not farre from this, there stands on little mount,
A right fayre Church, with pillars large and wide:
A monument, therein of good account,
Full finely wrought, amid the Quéere I spyde,
A Tombe there is, right rich and stately made,
Where two doth lye, in stone and auncient trade.

L 3   The

Keeryock a wondrous violent water.

Maister Iohn Edwards hath a fayre house nere this.

Newe Bridge on the Riuer Dee.

A straûge nature of a water

There is a poole in Meryonethshiere of three myle long rageth so by storme that it makes this Riuer flowe.

Ruabon Church is a fayre peece of worke.

The man and wife, with sumptuous sollemne guyse,
In this rich sort, before the Aulter lyes.

This Gentleman was called Iohn Bellis Eytton.

His head on crest, and warlike Helmet stayes,
A Lyon blew, on top thereof comes out:
On Lyons necke, along his legges he layes,
Two Gauntlets white, are lying there about.
An auncient Squire, he was and of good race,
As by his Armes, appæres in many a place:
His house and lands, not farre from thence doth shoe,
His birth and blood, was great right long agoe.

The trimmest glasse, that may in windowe bée,
(Wherein the roote, of Iesse well is wrought)
At Aulter head, of Church now shall you see,
Yea all the glasse, of Church was déerely bought.

Offaes Dyke.

Within two myles, there is a famous thing,
Cal'de Offaes Dyke, that reacheth farre in length:
All kind of ware, the Danes might thether bring,
It was free ground, and cal'de the Britaines strength.

Wats Dyke.

Wats Dyke likewise, about the same was set,
Betwéene which two, both Danes and Britaines met,
And trafficke still, but passing bounds by sleight,
The one did take, the other prisner streight.

Thus foes could méete, (as many tymes they may)
And doe no harme, when profite ment they both:
Good rule and lawe, makes baddest things to stay,
That els by rage, to wretched reuell goeth.
The brutest beasts, that sauage are of kynd,
Together comes, as season is assynde:
The angryest men, that can no friendship byde,
Must ceace from warre, when peace appalles their pride.

Now

# of Wales.

Now let this goe, and call in haſte to minde,
Trim Wrickſam Towne, a pearle of Denbighſhiere:
In whoſe fayre Church, a Tombe of ſtone I finde,
Under a wall, right hand on ſide of Quére.
On th'other ſide, one Pilſon lyes in graue,
Whoſe hearſe of blacke, ſayth he a Tombe ſhall haue:
In Quére lyes Hope, by Armes of gentle race,
Of function once, a rector in that place.

But ſpeake of Church, and ſtéple as I ought,
My pen to baſe, ſo fayre a worke to touch:
Within and out, they are ſo finely wrought,
I cannot praiſe, the workmanſhip too much.
But buylt of late, not eight ſcore yéeres agoe,
Not of long tyme, the date thereof doth ſhoe:
No common worke, but ſure a worke moſt fine,
As though they had, bin wrought by power deuine.

The ſtéple there, in forme is full foure ſquare,
Yet euery way, fiue pinnackles appére:
Trim Pictures fayre, in ſtone on outſide are,
Made all like waxe, as ſtone were nothing dére.
The height ſo great, the breadth ſo bigge withall,
No peece thereof, is likely long to fall,
A worke that ſtands, to ſtayne a number more,
In any age, that hath bin buylt before.

❧ A generall Commenda-
tion of Gentilitie.

NEre Wrickſam dwels, of Gentlemen good ſtore,
Of calling ſuch, as are right well to liue:
By Market towne, I haue not ſeene no more,
(In ſuch ſmall roume) that auncient Armes doe giue.

Robert Ho-
well lyes there
a Gentleman.

In Maylor, are all these Gentlemen.

Maister Roger Pilsons house at Irchley.

Maister Almmer at Pantyokin.

Maister Iohn Pilson of Bersan.

Maister Edward Iones of Cadoogan.

Maister Iames Eaton of Eatton.

Maister Edward Eaton by Ruabon.

Maister Owen Brueton of Borras.

Maister Iohn Pilson of Haberdewerne.

Maister Thomas Powell of Horsley.

Maister Iohn Treuar of Trenolin.

A gene all praise of all Gentlemen inhabiting of any Countrey.

They are the ioye, and gladnesse of the poore,
That dayly feedes, the hungrie at their doore:
In any Soyle, where Gentlemen are found,
Some house is kept, and bountie doth abound.

They beautifie, both Towne and Countrey too,
And furnisht are, to serue at neede in feeld:
And euery thing, in rule and order do,
And vnto God, and man due honour yeeld.
They are the strength, and suretie of the Land,
In whose true hearts, doth trust and credit stand,
By whose wise heads, the neighbours ruled are,
In whom the Prince, reposeth greatest care.

They are the flowers, of euery garden ground,
For where they want, there growes but wicked weedes:
Their tree and fruite, in rotten world is sownd,
Their noble mynds, will bring foorth faithfull deedes:
Their glorie rests, in Countries wealth and fame,
They haue respect, to blood and auncient name:
They weigh nothing, so much as loyall hart,
Which is most pure, and cleane in euery part.

They doe vphold, all ciuill maners myld,
All manly acts, all wise and woorthie waies:
If they were not, the Countrey would grow wyld,
And we should soone, forget our elders daies:
Ware blunt of wit, in speech growe rude and rough,
Want vertue still, and haue of vice enough.
Shewe feeble spieete, lacke courage euery where,
Dout many a thing, and our owne shadowes feare.

They dare attempt, for fame and hye renowne,
To scale the Clowdes, if men might clyme the ayre:
Assault the Starres, and plucke the Planets downe,
Giue charge on Moone, and Sunne that shines so fayre.

# of Wales.

I meane they dare, attempt the greatest things,
Flye swiftly ore, high Hilles if they had wings:
Beate backe the Seas, and teare the Mountaines too,
Yea what dare not, a man of courage doo.

Now must I turne, to my discourse agayne,
I Wricksam leaue, and pen out further place:
So if my muse, were now in pleasant vayne,
Holt Castle should, from verse receiue some grace:
The Seate is fine, and trimly buylt about,
With lodgings fayre, and goodly roumes throughout,
Strong Vaults and Caues, and many an old deuice,
That in our daies, are held of worthie price.

That place must passe, with praise and so adue,
My muse is bent, (and pen is readie prest)
To feede your eares, with other matters newe,
That yet remaines, in head and labouring brest.
A Mountaine towne, that is Thlangothlan calde,
A prettie Seate, but not well buylt nor walde,
Stands in the way, to Yale and Writhen both,
Where are great Hilles, and Plaines but fewe for troth.

Of Mountaines now, in deede my muse must runne,
The Poets there, did dwell as fables sayne:
Because some say, they would be neere the Sunne,
And taste sometymes, the frost, the cold, and rayne,
To iudge of both, which is the chiefe and best.
Who knowes no toyle, can neuer skill of rest,
Who alwaies walkes, on carpet soft and gay,
Knowes not hard Hilles, nor likes the Mountaine way.

A discourse of Mountaynes.

Dame Nature drew, these Mountaynes in such sort,
As though the one, should yeld the other grace:

M

Holt Castle
an excellent
fine place, the
Riuer of Dee
running by it.

Maister H...e
dwelles there.

Mai...'s ...r...
Hu... dwelles
in Y... in a
fayre ...

Castle Dy-
nosebraen on
a wooddie hill
on the one
side, & Greene
Castle on the
other.

A Bridge of
stone very faire
there stands
ouer Dee.

Maister La-
kon.
Ma. Thlude
of Yale.

D₂

The worthines

Oz as each Hill,it selfe were such a Fozt,
They scoznde to stowpe,to giue the Cannon place,
If all were playne,and smooth like garden ground,
Where should hye woods,and goodly groues be found?
The eyes delight,that lookes on euerp coast,
With pleasures great,and fayze pzospect were lost.

On Hill we vewe,farre of both feeld and flood,
Feele heate oz cold,and so sucke vp swæte ayze:
Behold beneath,great wealth and wozldly good,
Sæ walled Townes,and looke on Countries fayze,
And who so sits,oz stands on Mountayne hye,
Hath halfe a wozld,in compasse of his eye:
A platfozme made,of Nature foz the nonce,
Where man map looke,on all the earth at once.

These ragged Rocks,bzings playnest people foozth,
On Mountaine wyld,the hardest Hozse is bzed:
Though grasse thereon,be grosse and little wozth,
Swæte is the foode,where hunger so is fed.
On rootes and hearbs,our fathers long did feede,
And nære the Skye,growes swæest fruit in dæde:
On marrish meares,and watrie mossie ground,
Are rotten wædes,and rubbish dzosse vnsound.

The fogges and mists,that rise from vale belowe,
A reason makes,that highest Hilles are best:
And when such fogges,doth oze the Mountayne goe,
In foulest daies,fayze weather map be gest.
As bitter blasts,on Mountaynes bigge doth blowe,
So noysome smels,and sauours bzeede belowe:
The Hill stands clære,and cleaue from filthie snell,
They finde not so,that doth in Valley dwell.

The Mountayne men,liue longer manp a yære,
Then those in Vale,in playne oz marrish soyle:

A luſtie hart,a cleane complexion clære
They haue on Hill, that for hard liuing toyle,
VVith Ewe and Lambe,with Goates and Kids they play,
In greateſt toyles, to rub out wearie day:
And when to houſe,and home good fellowes drawe,
The lads can laugh,at turning of a ſtrawe.

No ayre ſo pure,and wholeſome as the Hill,
Both man and beaſt,delights to be thereon:
In heate or cold,it kæpes one nature ſtill,
Trim neate and drye,and gay to go vpon.
A place moſt fit,for paſtime and good ſport,
To which wyld Stagge,and Bucke doth ſtill reſort:
To crye of Hounds,the Mountayne ecco yælds,
A grace to Uale,a beautie to the feelds.

It ſtands for world,as though a watch it were,
A ſtately gard,to kéepe greene meddowe myld:
The Poets fayne, on ſhoulders it doth beare
The Heauens hye,but there they are beguyld.
The maker firſt,of Mountayne and of Uale,
Made Hill a wall,to clip about the Dale:
A ſtrong defence,for nædfull fruit and Corne,
That els by blaſt,might quickly be forlorne.

If boyſtrous wynds,were not withſtood by ſtrength,
Repulſt by force, and driuen backward too,
They would deſtroy,our earthly ioyes at length,
And through their rage,they would much miſchiefe doo.
God ſawe what ſmart,and griefe the earth would byde
By ſturdie ſtormes,and pearcing tempeſts pryde:
So Mountaynes made,to ſaue the lower ſoyle,
For feare the earth,ſhould ſuffer ſhamefull ſpoyle.

How could weake leaues,and bloſſomes hang on tree,
If boyſtring wynds,ſhould braunches dayly beate:

How

The worthines

How could poore soules, in Cottage quiet bee,
If higher grounds, did not defend their seate.
Who buylds his bower, right vnder feate of hill,
Hath little cold, and weather warme at will:
Thus proue I here, the Mountaine frendeth all,
Stands stiffe gaynst Stormes, like steele or brazen wall.

You may compare, a King to Mountayne hye,
Whose princely power, can byde both brunt and shocke
Of bitter blast, or Thunderbolt from Skye,
His Fortresse stands, vpon so firme a Rocke.
A Prince helps all, and doth so strongly sit,
That none can harme, by fraude, by force nor wit.
The weake must leane, where strength doth most remayne,
The Mountayne great, commaunds the little Playne.

As Mountayne is, a noble stately thing,
Thrust full of stones, and Rocks as hard as steele:
A peereles peece, comparde vnto a King,
Who sits full fast, on top of Fortunes wheele:
So is the Dale, a place of suttle ayre,
A den of drosse, oft tymes more foule then fayre:
A durtie Soyle, where water long doth byde,
Yet ritch withall, it cannot be denyde.

But wealth mars wit, and weares out vertue cleane,
An eating worme, a Cancker past recure:
A trebble loude, but not a merrie meane,
That Musick makes, but rather iarres procure:
A stirrer vp, of strife and leaud debate,
The ground of warre, that stayneth euery state
With giftes and bribes, that greedie glutton feedes
And filles the gut, whereon great treason breedes.

Wealth fosters pride, and heaues vp haughtie hart,
Makes wit oreweene, and man beleeue to farre:

Enfects

Enfects the mynd, with vice in euery part,
That quickly sets, the sences all at warre.
In Valley ritch, these mischiefes nourisht are,
God planted peace, on Mountayne poore and bare:
By sweat of browes, the people liues on Hill,
Not sleight of brayne, ne craft nor cunning skill.

Where dwels disdayne, discord or dubble waies,
But where ritch Cubs, and currish Carles are found:
Where is more loue, who hath more happie daies,
Then those poore hynds, that digges and delues the ground.
Perhaps you say, so hard the Rocks may bee,
Ne Corne nor grasse, nor plough thereon you see:
Yet loe the Lord, such blessing there doth giue,
That sweet content, with Oten Cakes can liue.

Sowre Whey and Curds, can yeeld a sugred tast,
Where sweete Martchpane, as yet was neuer knowne:
When emptie gorge, hath bole of Milke embrast,
And Cheese and bread, hath dayly of his owne,
He craues no feast, nor seekes no banquets fine,
He can digest, his dinner without wine:
So toyles out life, and likes full well this trade,
Not fearing death, because his count is made.

Who sleepes so sound, as he that hath no Sheepe,
Nor heard of Beasts, to pastor and to feede:
Who feares the Wulfe, but he who Lambes doth keepe,
And many an hower, is forst to watch in deede.
Though gold be gay, and cordiall in his kynd,
The losse of wealth, grypes long a greedie mynd,
Poore Mountayne folke, possesse not such great store,
But when its gon, they care not much therefore.

M 3   Of

The worthines
Of Yale a little to
be spoken of.

The names of
the Riuers of
Denbighshire.
Keeriock parts
Shropshere &
Denbighshere,
before Chirk.
Dee at newe
Bridge, and
Thlangoth-
len.
Aleyn in the
valley of Yale.
Clanweddock
in the fayre
vale of Dustin
Cloyd.
Cloyd receiues
Clanweddock
and Elwye by
Saint Affe.
Istrade by
Denbigh.
Rathad comes
to the Voin-
ney.
Keynthleth
comes into
Raykad.

THE Countrie Yale, hath Hilles and Mountaynes hye,
 Small Valleys there, saue where the Brookes do ron:
So many Springs, that fielb that soyle is drye:
God Turffe and Peate, on mossie ground is won,
Wherewith god fires, is made for man most meete,
That burneth cleere, and yeelds a sauour sweete
To those which haue, no nose for dayntie smell,
The finer sort, were best in Court to dwell.

This Soyle is cold, and subiect vnto winde,
Hard duskie Rocks, all couered ore full dim:
Where if winde blowe, ye shall foule weather finde,
And thinke you feele, the bitter blasts full brim.
But though cold bytes, the face and outward skin,
The stomacke loe, is thereby warm'd within.
For still more meate, the Mountayne men disgest,
Then in the playne, you finde among the best.

Here is hard waies, as earth and Mountayne yeelds,
Some softnesse too, as tract of foote hath made:
But to the Dames, for walke no pleasant feelds,
Nor no great wods, to shroud them in the shade.
Yet Sheepe and Goates, are plentie here in place,
And god welsh Nagges, that are of kindest race:
With godly nowt, both fat and bigge with bone,
That on hard Rocks, and Mountayne feedes alone.

Of Wrythen now, I treate as reason is,
But lisence craue, to talke on such a Seate:
Excuse my skill, where pen or muse doth mis,
Where knowledge fayles, the cunning is not great.

But

But ere I write, a verse vpon that Soyle,
I will crye out, of Tyme that all doth spoyle:
As age weares youth, and youth giues age the place,
So Tyme weares world, and doth old works disgrace.

A discourse of Tyme.

O Tract of Tyme, that all consumes to dust,
We hold thee not, for thou art bald behinde:
The fayrest Sword, or mettall thou wilt rust,
And brightest things, bring quickly out of minde.
The trimmest Towers, and Castles great and gay,
In processe long, at length thou doest decay:
The brauest house, and princely buildings rare,
Thou wasts and weares, and leaues the walles but bare.

O Cancker vyle, that creepes in hardest mold,
The Marble stone, or Flint thy force shall feele:
Thou hast a power, to pearce and eate the gold,
Fling downe the strong, and make the stout to reele.
O wasting worme, that eates sweete kernels all,
And makes the Nut, to dust and powder fall:
O glutton great, that feedes on each mans store,
And yet thy selfe, no better art therefore.

Tyme all consumes, and helps it selfe no whit,
As fire by flame, burnes coales to sinders small:
Tyme steales in man, much like an Agew fit,
That weares the face, the flesh the skinne and all.
O wretched rust, that wilt not scoured bee,
O dreadfull Tyme, the world is feard of thee:
Thou flingest flat, the highest Tree that growes,
And tryumph makes, on pompe and paynted showes.

But most of all, my muse doth blame thee now,
For throwing downe, a rare and goodly Seate:

By

By Wrythen Towne, anoble Castle throwe,
That in tyme past, had many a loging greate,
And Towers most fayre, that long a t upiding was,
Where now God wot, there grewes nothing but grasse:
The stones lye waste, the walles seemes but a shell
Of little worth, where once a Prince might dwell.

Of Wrythen, both the Castle
and the Towne.

The Castle of Wrythen is yet outwardly a marueilous faire and large princely place.

This Castle stands, on Rocke much like red Bricke,
   The Dykes are cut, with toole through stonie Cragge:
The Towers are hye, the walles are large and thicke,
The worke it selfe, would shake a Subiects bagge,
If he were bent, to buyld the like agayne:
It rests on mount, and lookes o're wood and Playne:
It had great store, of Chambers finely wrought,
That tyme alone, to great decay hath brought.

It shewes within, by dubble walles and waies,
A deepe deuice, did first erect the same:
It makes our world, to thinke on elders daies,
Because the worke, was founde in such a frame.
One tower or wall, the other answers right,
As though at call, each thing should please the sight:
The Rocke wrought round, where euery tower doth stand,
Set foorth full fine, by head by hart and hand.

There is a Poole here abouts that hath in it a kynd of fish that no other water can shewe.

And fast hard by, runnes Cloyd a Riuer swift,
In winter tyme, that swelles and spreads the feeld:
That water sure, hath such a secret gift,
And such rare Fish, in season due doth yeeld,
As is most straunge: let men of knowledge now:
Of such his cause, search out the nature throwe:

# of VVales.

A Poole there is, through which this Cloyd doth passe,
Where is a Fish, that some a Whiting call:
Where neuer yet, no Sammon taken was,
Yet hath good store, of other Fishes all
Aboue that Poole, and so beneath that flood
Are Sammons caught, and many a Fish full good:
But in the same, there will no Sammon bee,
And neere that Poole, you shall no Whiting see.

I haue left out, a Riuer and a Uale,
And both of them, are fayre and worthie note:
Who will them seeke, shall finde them still in Yale,
They beare such fame, they may not be forgot.
The Riuer runnes, a myle right vnder ground,
And where it springs, the issue doth abound:
And into Dee, this water doth dissend,
So loseth name, and therein makes an end.

A Riuer called Aleyn, in the valley of Yale.

Good ground likewise, this Ualley seemes to bee,
And many a man, of wealth is dwelling there:
On Mountayne top, the Ualley shall you see
All ouer greene, with goodly Meddowes feare.
This Ualley hath, a noble neighbour neere,
Wherein the Towne, of Wrythen doth appeere:
Which Towne stands well, and wants no pleasant ayre,
The noble Soyle, and Countrey is so fayre.

The valley of Yale.

A Church there is, in Wrythen at this day,
Wherein Lord Gray, that once was Earle of Kent,
In Tombe of stone, amid the Chauncell lay:
But since remou'd, as worldly matters went,
And in a wall, so layd as now he lyes
Right hand of Quære, full playne before your eyes:
An Anckres too, that nere that wall did dwell,
With trim wrought worke, in wall is buryed well.

The Earle of Kent lyes here.

An Anckres in King Henrie the fourths tyme buryed here.

N   Now

The worthines

Now to the Uale, of worthie Dyffrin Cloyd,
My muse must passe, a Soyle most ritch and gay:
This noble Seate, that neuer none anoyd,
That sawe the same, and rode or went that way:
The vewe thereof, so much contents the mynd,
The ayre therein, so wholesome and so kynd:
The beautie such, the breadth and length likewise,
Makes glad the hart, and pleaseth each mans eyes.

The pleasant vale of Diffrin Cloyd.

This Uale doth reach, so farre in vewe of man,
As he farre of, may see the Seas in deede:
And who a while, for pleasure trauayle can
Throughout this Uale, and thereof take good heede,
He shall delight, to see a Soyle so fine,
For ground and grasse, a passing plot deuine.
And if the troth, thereof a man may tell,
This Uale alone, doth all the rest excell.

As it belowe, a wondrous beautie showes,
The Hilles aboue, doth grace it trebble fold:
On euery side, as farre as Ualley goes,
A border bigge, of Hilles ye shall behold:
They kéepe the Uale, in such a quiet sort,
That birds and beasts, for succour there resort:
Yea flocks of foule, and heards of beasts sometyme,
Drawes there from storme, when tempests are in pryme.

The Vale throughly described.

Thrée Riuers run, amid the bottome heere,
Istrade, and Cloyd, Clanweddock (loe) the third:
The noyse of streames, in Sommer morning cléere,
The chirp and charme, and chaunt of euery bird
That passeth there, a second Heauen is:
No hellish sound, more like an earthly blis:
A Musick sweete, that through our eares shall creepe,
By secret arte, and lull a man a sleepe.

Three Riuers in this Vale.

A naturall secret touched.

The

The Castle of Cargoorley
in Denbighshiere,

Cargoorley comes, right now to passe my pen,
With ragged walles, yea all to rent and torne:
As though it had, bin neuer knowne to men,
Or carelesse left, as wretched thing forlorne:
Like begger bare, as naked as my nayle,
It lyes along, whose wracke doth none bewayle.
But if she knewe, to whom it doth pertayne,
What royalties, and honors doth remayne
Unto that Seate, it should repayred bee,
For further cause, then common people see.

But sondrie things, that are full farre from sight,
Are out of mynd, and cleane forgot in fine:
So such as haue, thereto but little right,
Possesse the same, by leauell and by line,
Or els by hap, or suite as often falles:
But what of that, Cargoorleys rotten walles
Can neuer bring, his betters in dispute,
That hath perchaunce, bin got by hap or sute:
So rest good muse, and speake no further heere,
Least by these words, some hidden thoughts appeere.

Kings giue and take, so tyme still rouleth on,
Good Subiects serue, for somewhat more or lesse:
And when we see, our fathers old are gon,
Of tyme to come, we haue a greater gesse.
First how to gayne, by present tyme and state,
Then what may fall, by futer tyme and date:
Tyme past growes cold, and so the world lukewarme
Doth helpe it selfe, by Castle, house or Farme:
That reach is good, that rule my frends God send,
Which well begin, and makes a vertuous end.

Thomas Sa-
lesburie of
Lleweni.
Robert Sales-
burie of Ba-
chenbid.
Foulk Lloyd
of Houllan.
Piers Holland
of Kynmel.
Piers Owen of
Abergele.
Edward The-
keall of Beren.
William Wyn
of Llamuaire.
Elis Price of
Spitty.
Iohn Middle-
ton.

The worthines

O Denbigh now, appeare thy turne is next,
    I néede no gloſe, nor ſhade to ſet thée out:
For if my pen, doe followe playneſt text,
And paſſe next way, and goe nothing about,
Thou ſhalt be knowne, as worthie well thou art,
The nobleſt Soyle, that is in any part:
And for thy Seate, and Caſtle doe compare,
With any one, of Wales what ere they are.

The ſtrongeſt
Caſtle & ſeate
that euer man
beheld.

This Caſtle ſtands, on top of Rocke moſt hye,
A mightie Cragge, as hard as flint or ſtéele:
A maſſie mount, whoſe ſtones ſo déepe doth lye,
That no deuice, may well the bottome féele.
The Rocke diſcends, beneath the auncient Towne,
About the which, a ſtately wall goes downe,
With buyldings great, and poſternes to the ſame,
That goes through Rocke, to giue it greater fame.

Marke wel the
ſituation and
buylding of
the ſame.

I want good words, and reaſons apt therefore,
It ſelfe ſhall ſhewe, the ſubſtance of my tale:
But yet my pen, muſt tell here ſomewhat more,
Of Caſtles praiſe, as I haue ſpoke of Vale.
A ſtrength of ſtate, ten tymes as ſtrong as fayre,
Yet fayre and fine, with dubble walles full thicke,
Like tarres trim, to take the open ayre,
Made of Fréeſtone, and not of burned Bricke:
No buylding there, but ſuch as man might ſay,
The worke thereof, would laſt till Iudgement day.

The Seate ſo ſure, not ſubiect to a Hill,
Nor yet to Myne, nor force of Cannon blaſt:
Within that houſe, may people walke at will,
And ſtand full ſafe, till daunger all be paſt.
If Cannon rorde, or barkt againſt the wall,
Frends there may ſay, a figge for enemies all:
Fiue men within, may kéepe out numbers greate,
(In furious ſort) that ſhall approach that Seate.

Whe

Who ſtands on Rocke, and lokes right downe alone,
Shall thinke belowe, a man is but a child:
I ſought my ſelfe, from top to fling a ſtone
With full mayne foꝛce, and yet I was beguyd.
If ſuch a height, the mightie Rocke be than,
Ne foꝛce noꝛ ſleight, noꝛ ſtout attempt of man,
Can win the Foꝛt, if houſe be furniſht thꝛow,
The troth whereof, let woꝛld be witneſſe now.

A practiſe by the Authoꝛ proued.

It is great payne, from fote of Rocke to clyme
To Caſtle wall, and it is greater toyle
On Rocke to goe, yea any ſtep ſometyme
Upꝛightly yet, without a faule oꝛ foyle.
And as this Seate, and Caſtle ſtrongly ſtands,
Paſt winning ſure, with engin ſwoꝛd oꝛ hands:
So lokes it oꝛe, the Countrey farre oꝛ neere,
And ſhines like Toꝛch, and Lanterne of the Sheere.

A great glorie giuen to Denbigh.

Wherefoꝛe Denbigh, thou bearſt away the pꝛaiſe,
Denbigh hath got, the garland of our daies:
Denbigh reapes fame, and lawde a thouſand waies,
Denbigh my pen, vnto the Clowdes ſhall raiſe.
The Caſtle there, could I in oꝛder dꝛawe,
It ſhould ſurmount, now all that ere I ſawe.

¶ Of Valey Crucis Thlangothlan, and
the Caſtle Dynoſebrane.

THE great deſire, to ſee Denbigh at full,
 Did dꝛawe my muſe, from other matter true:
But as that ſight, my mynd away did pull
From foꝛmer things, I ſhould pꝛeſent to you.
So duetie bids, a wꝛiter to be playne,
And things left out, to call to mynd agayne:
Thlangothlan then, muſt yet come once in place,
Foꝛ diuers notes, that giues this boke ſome grace.

Au

The worthines

An Abbey nére, that Mountayne towne there is,
Whose walles yet stand, and steeple two likewise:
But who that rides, to'see the troth of this,
Shall thinke he mounts, on hilles vnto the Skyes.
For when one hill, behind your backe you see,
Another comes, two tymes as hye as hee:
And in one place, the Mountaynes stands so there,
In roundnesse such, as it a Cockpit were.

The Abbey of Valey Crucis.

Their height is great, and full of narrowe waies,
And stéepe downe right, of force ye must descend:
Some houses are, buylt there but of late dayes,
Full vnderneath, the monstrous Mountaynes ende
Amid them all, and those as man may gesse,
When rayne doth fall, doth stand in sore distresse:
For mightie streames, runnes ore both house and thatch,
When for their liues, poore men on Hilles must watch.

Beyond the same, and yet on Hill full hye,
A Castle stands, an old and ruynous thing:
That haughtie house, was buylt in weathers eye,
A pretie pyle, and pleasure for a King.
A Fort, a Strength, a strong and stately Hold
It was at first, though now it is full old:
On Rocke alone, full farre from other Mount
It stands, which shewes, it was of great account.

Castle Dynosebraen.

Betwéene the Towne, and Abbey built it was,
The Towne is nére, the goodly Riuer Dée,
That vnderneath, a Bridge of stone doth passe,
And still on Rocke, the water runnes you see
A wondrous way, a thing full rare and straunge,
That Rocke cannot, the course of water chaunge:
For in the streame, huge stones and Rocks remayne,
That backward might, the flood of force constrayne.

A goodly bridge of stone here. The Towne and the bridge with the vyolent Riuer before that Towne.

From

From thence to Chirke, are Mountaynes all a rowe,
As though in ranke, and battaile Mountaynes stood:
And ouer them, the bitter winde doth blowe,
And whirles betwixt, the valley and the wood.
Chirke is a place, that parts another Sheere,
And as by Trench, and Mount doth well appeere:
It kept those bounds, from forrayne force and power,
That men might sleepe, in suretie euery hower.

Here Denbighshiere, departs from writers pen,
And Flintshiere now, comes brauely marching in,
With Castles fine, with proper Townes and men,
Whereof in verse, my matter must begin:
Not for to fayne, and please the tender eares,
But to be playne, as worlds eye witnesse beares:
Not by heresay, as fables are set out,
But by good proofe, of vewe to bryd a bout.

A little spoke of Flintshiere.

The Author fell sicke here.

When Sommer sweete, hath blowne ore Winters blast,
And waies ware hard, that now are soft and foule:
When calmie Skyes, sayth bitter stormes are past,
And Clowdes ware cleere, that now doth lowre and skoule,
My muse I hope, shall be reuiu'de againe,
That now lyes dead, or rockt a sleepe with paine.
For labour long, hath wearied so the wit,
That studious head, a while in rest must sit:
But when the Spring, comes on with newe delite,
You shall from me, heare what my muse doth write.

The writer takes here breath till a better season serues.

   Here endeth my first booke of the worthines of Wales: which
being wel taken, wil encourage me to set forth another: in which
worke, not only the rest of the Shieres (that now are not written
of) shalbe orderly put in print, but likewise all ye auncient Armes
of Gentlemen there in general shalbe plainly described & set out,
to the open vewe of the world, if God permit me life and health,
towards the finishing of so great a labour.

FINIS.   Thomas Churchyard.

Churchuards   Armes.

EN·DIEV·   ET·MON   ROY·

www.ingramcontent.com/pod-product-compliance
Lightning Source LLC
Chambersburg PA
CBHW032154010726
47493CB00008BA/2689